INTO THE MEZZANINE

JOSHUA RAVEN

Red Ink. Publishing

First published in the UK by Blue Fish Publishing Limited in 2012. This edition published in the UK by Red Ink Publishing Limited, 2025.

© 2025 Red Ink Publishing Limited www.5fingers.co.uk

5fingers is a trademark of Red Ink Publishing Limited

This novel is a work of fiction. Names and characters are the product of the author's imagination and any resemblance to actual persons, living or dead, is entirely coincidental.

A catalogue record for this book is available from the British Library

Cover Design by JD Smith.

Title Production by The BookWhisperer

ISBN(eBook): 978-1-0685674-3-8
ISBN(Paperback): 978-1-0685674-4-5
ISBN(Hardcover): 978-1-0685674-5-2

This book is dedicated to my parents.
"Thank you" doesn't even begin to express my gratitude.

One finger one thumb keep moving
We'll all be merry and bright

 12345

CHAPTER 1

Lake Emerson rode the unicycle while juggling three Bowie knives. He grinned like a maniac, perspiring a little under his crimson headband. His life depended on him impressing his audience.

He cast the knives higher and higher into the air. As they twirled up and down, Lake caught them effortlessly by their short wooden handles. They were well-balanced and ideal for juggling, with nice, rounded points and brass cross-guards.

As he seized the lethal steel blades and tossed them back up, he kept his eyes on Stevie Teeth.

Stevie was the head of the Zodiacs, Griffton's home-grown brand of gang fraternity. The group comprised around thirty angry young boys. Many lived in squats or on the streets, and they were well known for being unpredictable and prone to senseless violence, smashing up trains, people, whatever.

Lake Emerson, the Griffton News reporter, was surrounded by a mob of Zodiacs. He was deep undercover. Like a secret agent, he had infiltrated their turf – it had taken stealth, guile, and a crate-load of guts.

Lake was researching a story that would either make his name as a writer or result in his death.

For the time being, he was as safe as he was going to be. Here he was, face to face with Stevie Teeth, a young man known for biting through peoples' ears if they looked at him the wrong way. Dark tales about him bubbled up from the underground from time to time, making parents blanch and mutter about the breakdown of society.

Flanking this disagreeable hooligan was a score of loyal followers. Several of them were, in truth, eager to kill Stevie and snatch his crown. But they were also very protective of their own ears. One thing was for sure, though; they all hated interlopers, and that's what Lake was: a spy.

If they got even one hint of a whiff that Lake was an investigative reporter, then right here, right now, in this cavernous warehouse on the outskirts of Griffton, it would be game over.

But right here, right now, Lake was the one with the knives.

He grinned and raised his eyebrows as the unicycle lurched backward. He left it until the very last minute to catch the knives as they cascaded towards his head.

Laughter exploded from Stevie. He nudged his number two, to whom everyone seemed to refer simply as Pig. Pig was even more disagreeable than Stevie, if that was possible, with a large wine-red face, huge hands, and a dirty laugh.

Pig swaggered and swore, calling out: "Go on, mate – let's see you cut your ears off!"

What is it with these people and ears? Lake thought as he edged towards his finale. With no warning and with practised incompetence, he made the unicycle lurch dangerously. Then he hurled the hunting knives high into the air and called, "One, two, three!" He squeezed his eyes shut and wrapped his head in his arms.

The Zodiacs loved the show.

LAKE COMPLETED his juggling display by vaulting off the unicycle just as the knives came tumbling down.

Once off, he executed a perfect backflip and landed squarely on his feet. The Bowie knives hit the floor of the warehouse and lay there. The crowd was a freeze-frame image of gawping, gaping, dirty-faced urchins with curry-coloured stains on their hooded tops.

Infiltrating the group had been easier than he'd thought. All he had to do was concoct a plausible hard-luck story, dress down, and mess up his hair. Oh, and sleep on the streets for a few days and roll in the dirt. That had definitely been the most unpleasant part of it all. He never knew so many bugs and spiders crawled the streets at night. But it had all helped to establish his new identity.

He was Micky McLaughlin, of no fixed abode. Unemployed but willing to do circus tricks for money. He was a runaway like so many of the Zodiacs. Micky had been travelling the country and decided to spend time by the sea. Griffton seemed as good a place as any to kick back and pass the time. There were plenty of Hawaiian-shirted tourists loaded with cash, and it was easy to draw a crowd at the beach with his circus tricks. Sometimes, they'd throw him money. Other times, he'd lift wallets. That's what he told them, anyway.

The Zodiacs had been convinced by the story. They stole him a unicycle, even finding him some batons and knives so he could entertain them in the evenings.

But four days into the charade, Lake was feeling distinctly nervy. One of the Zodiacs, a boy named Toby, had been taunting him quietly, trying to pick a fight. Lake suspected Toby was onto him.

They had been paired up for a job that day, Lake and Toby. They were watching a building on Griffton's west side for Stevie. They hadn't been told why they were surveying it, but it took most of the afternoon.

That was when Lake began to suspect Toby knew he was a

fake. The giveaway was when Toby remarked on Lake's "lovely fingernails and soft hands," sneering when he made the comments. Lake made a mental note to find mud to plunge his fingers into as soon as possible. He cursed the fact his hands had given him away. So much for his attention to detail.

During the juggling act, Lake saw Toby on his mobile phone when he should have been watching the show. He was sure he'd been rumbled.

Soon after, Toby moved over to Pig and whispered something, eyeing Lake as he talked. The Zodiacs rarely approached Stevie directly. Instead, they opted to send their comments through Pig. It partly meant the head Zodiac wasn't bothered by little things, but, more importantly, it protected them from Stevie's unpredictable moods.

From that moment on, Pig started watching Lake carefully. Lake tried to crack jokes and keep everyone amused, but his influence was ebbing away by the minute.

After the unicycle trick, the gang started to file out of the main doors of the warehouse. The only thing was, no one had told Lake where they were going.

Lake watched helplessly as he got left behind with Toby, Pig, and Stevie. One of the more friendly Zodiacs called out as he left, "Hey, Micky. We're going to get some pizzas downtown. You comin'?"

It was Robbie, a lanky Zodiac with thick, curly black hair and a lazy eye. He had been pleasant enough to Lake since he joined the gang, unlike some others. Lake had learned that Robbie himself was new and slept in the warehouse with a handful of Zodiacs who had been thrown out of their homes or had chosen to leave.

Pig stared hard at Lake and called out behind him, "Micky's just going to have a little chat with us. You go on, Rob. We'll catch up with you later."

Then he told Toby, "Why don't you go on ahead, dog? We'll finish up here."

Toby took one glance at Lake, bowed his head to Stevie, and left.

The noise of the young toughs receded. Lake was left in the abandoned warehouse on the north side of Griffton. He stood, legs apart, with the unicycle and blades strewn behind him. The place smelt like a mushroom farm. The grubby floor of the warehouse was littered with pants, socks, T-shirts, food packets, trainers, and weapons.

"So, what's the story, Micky McLaughlin?" spat Stevie. He wasn't laughing.

"Food sounds great. I'm hungry." Lake ran his hand through his hair, his mind racing. There was no way past these two guys. The broad warehouse doors had been pulled closed to give them privacy.

"Michael McLaughlin. Micky McLaughlin. Or should I say, Lake Emerson, news reporter on the Griffton News? That's right. We know who you are, bad boy."

Lake tried to swallow, but his throat had gone dry.

CHAPTER 2

"You don't look like no Zodiac. You don't even smell like no Zodiac. How long have you been living on the streets, eh? One week? And that scratch on your face. We reckon you did that yourself," sneered Stevie.

"And to think we let you in," growled Pig.

Then, they became deadly serious. "I'm hungry for some ears," said Stevie Teeth. There was no hint of humour in his voice or his expression. He stared hard at Lake, boring two holes into him with his dead eyes. Up close, these boys stank: the acrid odour rasped against Lake's throat. His rear taste buds usually enjoyed bitter tastes, particularly beer or Marmite, but this time, they did not relish the experience.

Lake knew he was thin on options.

He noticed Pig start to circle around him as Stevie stood stock-still. The time for talking was clearly over. Unless he acted fast, he was in big trouble.

Pig was gunning for one of the three hunting knives lying on the floor a little behind him.

Lake's gaze locked onto the unicycle. With a swift movement, he crouched low, his fingers curling around the lip of the seat while the other hand gripped the pole. In a fluid motion, his muscles coiled and then surged, lifting the unicycle off the ground with surprising ease.

Then he swung it, smacking Pig squarely on the jaw with the edge of the wheel. The surprise attack left him sprawled, his bulky body flat against the warehouse concrete. Lake dropped the unicycle and looked up, only to see Stevie looming over him.

Lake had another surprise attack in mind. He thrust both hands into his pockets and pulled something out of each. As he flung them forward, Stevie realised Lake was throwing sandy grit at his eyes. The speed of the attack was blinding, giving Lake the upper hand.

Yowling with rage, Stevie batted away the grit, but he was too late, and Lake was already racing to the exit.

"Give me a knife, Pig. I'm gonna gut him," shouted Stevie. "Call the others. I'm going after him."

Pig picked up a blade for Stevie and then pulled out his mobile phone. He hesitated while he dialled.

"You comin' or what?" shouted Stevie from the door. "He's getting away."

⤜ 12345 ⤛

LAKE FOUND himself in Rivet Place. It was an industrial business park with low flat-roofed buildings made of blue-grey concrete and unreflective metal. The garages and workshops in the complex mostly housed heavy machinery and vehicle parts.

He leaped over the oil patches outside the warehouse, knowing he had to keep moving. Escaping the Zodiacs only to be caught outside their headquarters was not a smart move.

It was now dark outside, but the security lights from the buildings kept the business park illuminated. Outside the estate, Lake could see yellow-orange streetlights dotted along the road. Freedom lay in that direction.

Pumped with adrenalin and fear, Lake ran for the exit. As he reached it, he suddenly changed his mind: it was too exposed on the main road. He'd quickly be spotted.

He stayed in the confines of Rivet Place and circled behind the buildings to the right. The Zodiac leaders would expect him to make a beeline for the main road and head for help or lose himself in Griffton's maze of streets. That was if he got there in time and they didn't outrun him. It was better to take his chances up here.

He waited, palms on knees, in the shadows of a low storehouse. Suddenly, he saw Stevie and Pig jogging to the large mouth of the business park.

They paused there, first taking a long look to their left, up the road, and then to the right, down toward the city. Then they nodded to each other. They started to trot down the hill into central Griffton, where the gang had gone for dinner.

Lake breathed deeply, safe at last. He padded stealthily from his hiding place to check the exit. Then he turned to examine the business park. It had a dozen or more grey buildings, some walled with corrugated metal and others smooth like marble.

He decided it was safe enough to grab his bag, which had his rollerblades, phone, and a couple of clothes inside. He had left it in the abandoned warehouse the Zodiacs used for a base.

In the building, Lake quickly found his possessions, laced up his blades, and slung the pack around his shoulder. He wore a pair of beaten-up old Roces. They hinted at long years of tricks and wipe-outs. But they also fitted in with his image of being a Zodiac. On the one hand, they were shabby and dirty. But on the other, they moved like lightning since he had upgraded the wheels and bearings. Lake grinned to himself, pleased to have his wheels on again.

A split second later, a figure sprang up and punched him to the ground, a burst of pain erupting at his temple.

Instinctively, Lake tucked into a skater's roll, his eyes locking onto the familiar face—it was Toby, his Zodiac partner. Toby, who had caught onto him earlier, taunted him throughout the day, and ultimately fed him to the gang leaders. Toby grabbed him by the leg and dragged him back into the building. He was incredibly strong. Lake groaned as his body scraped across the rough ground, thrashing wildly with his arms, but Toby was moving too fast. Although Toby was smaller and slighter than Lake, he was clearly tougher and more ruthless. Lake really didn't fancy his chances. He was sure Toby had a knife on him, at the very least.

Desperately, Lake cycled through his choices as quickly as he could. High on the list was to get up and race off. Taking Toby on in mortal combat was very low on the list. His best option was to engage his attacker in conversation and rely solely on his mouth. It had worked in the past. Not always, but most of the time.

"Listen, Toby, mate," he found himself burbling as he lay on the cold concrete floor in the massive shadowy warehouse, hidden from the glare of the security lights. "Do you like my skates?"

"What?" barked Toby.

"You can have 'em. I mean, they're a good pair, and they're really fast. I reckon they could fit you too if you had, like, really thin socks."

"Not interested. Anyway, if I was, they'd be mine already." Toby loomed menacingly over him.

Lake tried a different tack. "Toby, mate. You and me, we go back."

"What are you going on about?"

"I'm just saying. We had a great day today. And we're friends. It was nice getting to know you. So now we've got history, you and me."

"What history?"

Lake sighed and tried again. "Hey, you know, it's not a good idea to hurt me. I mean, you know who I am now. I'm Lake Emerson. I'm a famous news reporter for the biggest paper in the city. People love me. There's over a hundred thousand people read my paper. So, if you harm me, or, you know, kill me, then how's that going to look in black and white?" He stood up slowly, leaving Toby to think it over.

"I'd be a hero," said the Zodiac after a while.

"Thousands of people read my stories. Loads of people know my face."

"Does that make you better than me?"

Lake shook his head. "That's not what I'm saying, Toby."

"Well then, what?"

"Well, we both know you could do me some real harm, right?"

"Damn right. And don't you forget it, dog," Toby spat.

"Well, here's a radical suggestion. Why don't you let me go?"

"What?" spat the Zodiac. "You've got no idea how we work!"

"So, tell me."

"It's like this. We let you in. You broke the code. You're scum, and I have to kill you. Code of Honour."

"Look, Toby, mate. You don't have to kill me; you have so many options," laughed Lake.

"Like what?"

"Well, you could let me go," he suggested.

Toby made a growling noise from deep in his throat. Lake hastily added, "Or we could do an interview."

"A what?"

"Yeah, an interview for the Griffton News. You'd be famous, and I could, perhaps, show the gang in a more positive light? It would be good for all of us: a real no-brainer. A win-win. Everyone goes home happy."

"I don't wanna be famous," mumbled Toby.

"Course you do. Everyone wants to be famous."

"I need to call Pig." Toby reached for his mobile phone. "He'll know what to do."

"Oh, we don't need to involve them," whispered Lake. "You have more options. So many options. If you don't want to do an interview with me, that's fine. I personally think it's your best option by far. But, like I say, it's your decision. You could always let me go. Or else, you could pretend to beat me up and then maybe let me go?"

"Or, I could avenge the Zodiacs properly, Code of Honour, because you betrayed us, you middle-class scum. I could beat you up nice and leave you for dead."

Lake instantly regretted bringing up the subject of beatings as Toby's fist fell on his solar plexus, making him bend over double.

12345

AT TIMES LIKE THIS, Lake often thought about the mystery man who had appeared and rescued him and Rachel Race. It was a year ago, up on Griffton Cliff – a man-made quarry face that overlooked the city from the north.

The mystery man, Caleb Noble, had managed to remove doors from their hinges and completely lay out grown men without appearing to use any physical force. The guy was a legend. But it wasn't Caleb himself, the man had said. It was "the Dunamis," as though that explained everything. "My master sent him to give us power," Caleb had added. He had introduced them to this mysterious Dunamis as though he were calling forward a friend waiting at the back of the room.

The Dunamis truly felt like raw power — passion and purity combined, a weight on the emotions, an invisible river of adrenaline and tranquility. Lake had so many questions after that encounter. However, Caleb had to leave in a hurry, and that was that. They could never forget, though.

Caleb did tell them the Dunamis would protect them or something like that. He guessed that somehow that would help, particularly if they needed to dismantle a building.

He just wished he could understand what it all meant. In moments like these, he wished he had the guts to call on the Dunamis himself and be able to knock people out without even lifting a finger. But the truth was he couldn't do it — he was a realist. He must have been in some delusional state back then, he thought.

After all, he had been imprisoned in that old house by a bunch of nutter wizards and fed gruel for a week. It had been the darkest time in his whole life. Unless he had strong proof that any of the stuff with Caleb Noble happened in real life, he would find it awkward to call on the invisible to do the impossible. Even so, part of him could never forget the powerful presence of the Dunamis.

Another punch from Toby caught him off guard, sending him crashing to the floor again. The Zodiac yob was just starting to warm up; he grinned and started to fish out his mobile phone.

As Lake hit the ground, he suddenly remembered today was Rachel's birthday. Right about now, her friends would be getting ready for her birthday gathering at the Pirate's Paradise, their local pub. What was more, Lake was Rachel's boyfriend. If he didn't show up, it would be over between them.

He groaned.

CHAPTER 3

At last, the day had arrived. Rachel had been looking forward to her birthday party for a long time.

Now she was seventeen, Rachel could legally drive a car, buy an air rifle, or leave home without her parents' consent. She frequently thought about doing all three things, in that order: car, gun, gone.

Her dad, Eddie Race, was becoming a real weirdo. She still loved him, though distantly, like you love an old memory of a family holiday in the sun. It wasn't the sort of love a little girl has for her daddy or even that best friends have for one another.

He still did his plumbing and carpentry jobs in Griffton and Polcombe, but he said little about anything. He didn't eat much either and left all the food shopping to her, occasionally placing cash in the fruit bowl in the kitchen.

In fact, he pretty much left her alone and never even argued with her anymore. This was really strange because he'd always been quarrelsome and moody. Instead, he'd grown increasingly distant over the past year, and it was almost like they were housemates with nothing in common. They did their own thing, had their own friends, and went out to work separately. When they came home after work, the other one might be in, or they might not. Housemates like that catch up on the surface and talk about nothing: rubbish TV, the weather, food. That was the two of them.

Of course, they never talked about her mother. It was almost like his wife, Maryam—her mother—had never existed. But then again, perhaps she was a constant reminder of his loss. Every time she stared into the mirror, she saw more and more of her mother's features reflected in her own: the wide mouth, the big, serious brown eyes, and the long black eyelashes.

She couldn't really remember the last time she'd spent any significant time in a room with her father. But then again, she had been out and about more and more, partly to get away from him and partly because it was boring at home.

Most of the time, she was out doing one of her two jobs. The first was working at Rock and Shock, the record shop overlooking Griffton Beach, where she got to play all the music she liked. She could listen to new bands and watch music videos. Conversation with regulars and visitors was always fun. People-watching was one of her passions. She would always try to work out what music someone liked by how they dressed, even before they said anything. Mostly, she got it right.

She worked with Iona, who was her best friend now since Lara moved to California a year ago. She hadn't heard a whisper from her since – so much for their years of friendship. The thing that hurt the most was Lara hadn't even left her number or even an email address. They had been in and out of each other's houses throughout their teenage years, and now there was nothing.

Actually, it wasn't strictly true that Rachel hadn't heard a whisper from Lara. She had heard some snippets from Lake. He still kept in touch with Lara's brother, Joel, in the casual way that blokes do. At least Joel was still friends with Lake – it's all right for some. From those scant email exchanges, she had gleaned that Lara was now working in a beach café and had loads and loads of 'friends.' Well, that sounded typical of Los Angeles: everyone's your friend.

So anyway, Iona was her best pal now and did a superb job at being one. She cared about Rachel and tried to cheer her up when she was down. She asked interesting questions and listened hard to the answers, and Rachel tried to be just as good a friend.

Rachel's other job was at *Nightshift*, a publisher in the centre of town, where she did secretarial bits and pieces. It was okay work, lots of paper shuffling and phone calls. Nice people. The money was better than Rock and Shock, but she had no intention of leaving the record shop. Working there was too much fun.

When she wasn't working, she was usually out with Iona and her boyfriend, Lake. But that was another story altogether.

The first few months were great. He was so romantic, and they spent days together walking by the beach or up at Griffton Cliff. The summer was long and beautiful, with warm evenings and plenty of sunshine. Lake was funny and charming. She loved his handsome, square-jawed face and his treacle-coloured hair. He was very attentive and gave her lots of compliments and gifts. She even liked his jokes, painful though they were.

When it started to go wrong, it wasn't because of him. It really wasn't.

There was one time, up on the cliff, when she really should have been happy. He had surprised her with a gorgeous bunch of flowers, just like in the hospital the first time they met. It wasn't even a special occasion. They were turquoise and lavender and had elegant leafy-green sprigs of foliage.

"Oh, Lake, I'm speechless."

"Doesn't sound like it to me," he quipped.

They held hands as the orangey dusk approached and watched a mass of evening primroses open up, dazzling the evening with their canary-yellow faces. Evening primroses are like shy children who are fed an encouraging word. They quickly blossom, beaming with a new confidence. Similarly, the flowers burst open and stay open all night. It was just like Rachel and Lake's affection for each other: quick to bloom.

But evening primroses only live for a night once they have flowered. Rachel enjoyed Lake's company and his warmth as the night air started to cool. From that moment, something inside her began to crumble. It was her confidence. Why was he being so nice to her? Why her? What was so special about her? The thoughts tormented her, and her moods were all over the place. The road ahead was a rocky one for them.

He even tried asking about her mother. Big mistake. She didn't want to talk about it. But like the journalist he was becoming, he tried different approaches to open her up.

"What can you remember about your mum?" he asked.

When that didn't work, he tried a gentler approach. "Sometimes I find talking helps. It's good to talk about it."

Desperate, he even tried, "You're so beautiful and mysterious. Is that what she was like, too?"

But nothing worked because the subject was off-limits. Not that she didn't enjoy talking to him. She had been more open with him than she had ever been with any guy. The truth was she still didn't trust him with her innermost feelings. It had taken her a long time before she had talked to Lara about any of it. Then Lara betrayed her and dashed their friendship against the rocks.

Rachel knew she had a reputation for being emotional. Some people even called her a drama queen, even to her face. The reality was that ever since her mum had died suddenly when she was a little girl of nine, she just hadn't been able to keep it together for long. It was hard, but somehow, she had gotten used to this massive range of emotions: wild laughter, dark valleys of fear, and nights of weeping. It was what she was used to, and she reckoned she would always be that way: an emotionally broken basket case. She could never be healed of it.

Her coldness towards Lake was mainly because of her own damage, but Rachel was well aware of it. Eventually, she started to push him away. They were still boyfriend and girlfriend; he wanted that more than her, hoping she would come back around. But she couldn't stop herself from becoming detached. The thing was, how could anyone love her? After all, her mother had died in front of her in the kitchen, and she had done nothing to stop it.

❧ *12345* ❧

As Rachel was getting ready for her birthday night out, the doorbell rang. She opened the door to find a petite Japanese girl with shoulder-length black hair smothered in Hello Kitty accessories and floral perfume.

"Yes?" said Rachel, surprised. She rarely had visitors, and certainly not anyone like this. Maybe she was selling something —perfume or makeup, by the looks of it.

"I'm looking for Lake. Is he here?" She was around the same age as Rachel, or perhaps older, with a round, compact face and the eyes of a cat.

"Who's asking?"

"Mrs Emerson said he might be here. You're his friend, right?" She had a broad Australian accent, which kind of threw Rachel. Or was it New Zealand? She had pronounced "friend" as "freend."

"I am. And who are you?"

"I'm Kumiko. I'm Lake's fiancée."

CHAPTER 4

Rachel realised her mouth was hanging open, so she quickly closed it. Then she said flatly, "You have got to be kidding me."

"I'm Kumiko, but you can call me Kumi," sang the girl.

"Kumi? Okay, nice to meet you, I suppose," she heard herself saying. "I'm Rachel, a friend of Lake's."

Rachel felt her heart start to power down like a computer slipping into sleep mode. She was battening down the hatches to weather the storm. *Lake has a fiancée? When did that happen? Where did she come from? How come he never mentioned that?* She would definitely have remembered. Rachel found herself smiling, but there were tears in her eyes. Why hadn't she said she was Lake's girlfriend? Why just his 'friend'?

How long had she known him? Little more than a year. It was entirely possible he'd had a long-term relationship before her. Maybe he and this girl had dated since he was fifteen. They could easily have become engaged after a couple of years. Then, somehow, he had stashed her away for a year until he was ready for marriage, all while toying with Rachel's heart. Rachel felt sick but tried to make her face unreadable.

Kumi grinned a cute and girlish grin and twisted shyly on

her ankles, shifting from one side to the other. She looked at Rachel all the while with her cat-like eyes. Rachel noticed the girl's Hello Kitty Princess top matched her handbag and belt. She had clearly put a lot of thought into her outfit.

"Look, I'm meeting him at the Pirate's Paradise later tonight. Do you know it?"

"Down at the beach? Yes."

"He'll be there. It's my birthday."

"Oh, Happy Birthday, Rachel!"

Kumi left, leaving a cloud of perfume behind her. She gave a small wave of her fingers as she walked away. This small stranger had arrived like a depth charge in Rachel's life.

Rachel closed the door and leaned back on it. "What is wrong with you? Why on earth did you invite her to your birthday party?" she scolded. "I need to talk to Iona. She'll know what to do."

Rachel quickly finished getting ready so that she could get over to Iona's. Then she sent her a hasty SOS text message: "Got a problem – coming over right now."

Iona was the friendship equivalent of sipping ice-cold lemonade on a hot summer's day or spotting a rainbow over Griffton Cliff. She was the silver lining around the cloud. Not that she tried to be positive and say the right thing. It was more like encouragement just oozed out of her. It was exactly what Rachel needed at this moment.

12345

THE BUS COULDN'T ARRIVE QUICKLY ENOUGH for Rachel. She leapt onto the curb and ran the distance to Iona's door with her heels clattering against the pavement.

In the past year, Iona's grandma had died and left her some money, so she had moved out of her little apartment in the centre of Griffton. The old place had been crammed full of coloured glass ornaments and bright furry rugs and had an aroma of tangerines. She was now living in a beautiful big house off Griffton Boulevard, on the west side.

The sea swelled outside her windows, and the buttercup-yellow sun bathed her in the mornings as she sipped hot, sweetened chai. She had traded the glass ornaments for rainbow textile wall hangings she'd made herself. The furry rugs had stayed, though, and were now littered with polka-dot beanbags. After a few days, this place smelled of tangerines, just like her last home.

"Don't you look lovely," cooed Iona as she opened the door to Rachel.

"Look who's talking!"

Rachel loved Iona. She was twenty-one, four years older than Rachel, and spoke in a breathy, girly-swirly voice. She always made up her own fashion, lacy dresses over rainbow leggings or tie-dye and ribbons with customised Dr Marten boots. Tonight, she wore a sky-blue tassel skirt, rainbow sandals, and a big-sleeved blouse. Her hair was up and tied with colourful ribbons.

Iona threw her arms around her friend. "Whatever the problem is, there's a solution," she said in her breathy voice.

"You reckon? This one might not be so easy."

"Well, let's see. Pull up a beanbag. I want to give you your birthday presents first."

Her presents from Iona were lovely. She had given her something useful (peppermint tea), something frivolous but fun (a fizzy lemon bath bomb), and something utterly bizarre (a 'gonk' troll doll with rainbow hair). It was all so 'Iona,' thought Rachel. She laughed and felt truly happy for the first time that evening. It was partly because Iona was grinning and because these were beautiful gifts she never would have bought herself. Not in a million years.

As for the Australian-Japanese girl, Iona's strategy was simple. They would stick together and see what happened when she turned up. It all hung on what Lake said and how he would explain it. That would tell her whether Rachel and Lake had a future or if it all ended tonight.

Lake was a great-looking guy, and Rachel knew he must have had past girlfriends hanging around, but a fiancée? That was unexpected.

⟢ 12345 ⟣

LAKE'S ARMS and legs stuck out awkwardly as he lay supine on the ground. The long, thick muscle on his side throbbed from the beating, and his back felt numb against the cold concrete.

Toby was perfectly happy waiting for backup. He whiled away the time by humming his favourite heavy rock tunes. Toby broke off occasionally and commented to Lake something like, "This one's 'Tears' by Candlemass. They're a Swedish doom-metal band. You should get yourself some."

Toby's phone conversation with Pig had been brief and gruff, punctuated by a series of grunts. The plan seemed to be that Toby would stand guard over Lake until the chiefs arrived to deliver their brand of justice personally. Lake was to be a sacrificial offering, and in exchange, Toby would receive some kind of Zodiac promotion. They were both thrown off guard when Lake's phone blared out a funky ditty. He had set the ring tone as a joke one day and liked it. It never failed to cheer him up, and today was no exception.

Lake eyed his bag and found himself grinning at the familiar noise that echoed around the empty warehouse. It was like a mewling baby demanding attention.

"I'd better get that."

"No. We ignore it," grunted Toby.

The phone refused to die but continued to warble from inside the rucksack. The funky dance tune rang out relentlessly, loud and proud. It declared to Toby in no uncertain terms, "I know watcha doin', I know watcha doin', boom-chukka-chuk, boom-chukka-chuk, I know watcha doin'!"

Toby started to twitch.

"I need to get it," said Lake sternly. "If I don't report back to my editor, he will call the police. The police will come to this warehouse. I told them where I was. What – you think I'd come out here and not tell anyone?" he lied.

Toby looked blank. He shot a glance at the bag, distracted by the funky ringtone. What was it? Stevie Wonder? Jackson 5? He couldn't quite work it out.

Seizing the moment, Lake pulled one knee up towards his chest and kicked out the toe of his rollerblade. The tough rubber wheels struck Toby hard between his legs. He howled like a wounded animal, his hands instinctively dropping to his groin.

Lake seized the valuable seconds he'd gained and scrambled to his feet. He only needed a moment more to grab his rucksack. Toby made a weak attempt to grab his arm, but Lake spun away with the grace and agility of a ballet dancer on wheels.

Then he speed-skated to the door.

"I wouldn't hang around," he called over his shoulder. "Feds are coming."

Bursting out of the warehouse, he launched himself off a low ramp and into the crisp night air. His wheels hit the concrete with a satisfying thud. "Sucker," he said, throwing the bag over a shoulder. He clutched his left side, which ached like a rotten tooth.

Head down, Lake raced out of Rivet Place and onto the streets of north Griffton. He was free at last.

➦ 12345 ➥

THE GREAT THING about skating in Griffton from north to south was that the roads sloped downwards towards the sea. As a skater, Lake had the advantage of speed if Toby chased him on foot. But without wheels, it was unlikely that Toby would catch him. No, Toby would need a car or, better still, a motorbike. Yeah, Lake was home-free, baby.

Griffton was a small city on the south coast of England with a nucleus of shops and public buildings in the centre, a cathedral, and a college. The nice houses were laid out beautifully on the west side, with the north also boasting its share of posh dwellings with superior views of the city and the sea. Lake lived towards the east side, level with the centre of town, and this was where he was heading now.

He lived with his parents, Blake and Anne, in a pleasantly furnished home with a long rectangular patch of garden and manicured rose bushes. After sleeping rough for the last few nights, he looked forward to sinking into his comfortable bed.

Lake thought he glimpsed Stevie Teeth with Pig and a couple of other Zodiacs down the road. But he couldn't be sure as he was skating so fast now. Taking no chances, he zipped over the road and disappeared into the side streets. He decided to approach his house from the east side of town and travelled on the smaller roads parallel to Roasting Vale Lane. The arterial road ran north to south until it collided with Griffton Boulevard, which ran east to west along the beach.

He calculated it was possible to make it home, have a wash, and still meet Rachel at the Pirate's Paradise by nine-thirty, saving his relationship.

"Piece of cake," he thought to himself. "It's all about hitting the deadlines."

⟡ 12345 ⟡

THE PIRATE'S Paradise had undergone a major refurbishment since last year. Rachel and her school friends had been going there for a couple of years now, and it had always been dingy, grungy, and down-at-heel, which was just how they liked it.

But now, Alan, the owner, had knocked out the sea-facing wall and turned the once cosy little pub into a more contemporary venue. The walls had gone from metallic anthracite grey to russet red and burnt umber, which was so Mediterranean.

Clichéd shell designs had even started to appear here and there. Alan had extended the outside seating area to the top of the beach and started to serve cocktails. He explained, with a shrug, that he needed to compete with the more modern chains that had invaded Griffton. Alan had also been granted a license to sell hot food, which had made the Pirate into more of a family gastro-pub.

Rachel supposed it was an improvement, but part of her pined for how it used to be. However, it was a lovely venue for a birthday gathering. They could share chips from a deep apricot-coloured bowl in the centre of the table and have a drink or two. It would be an evening to remember.

"There are still loads of people in the sea," said Iona.

"Don't you mean, 'plenty of fish in the sea'?"

"No, I mean the actual sea: over there– can you believe it? We could go for a dip later. Do you fancy it?" Iona's eyes were sparkling.

"You are joking?"

"No, I'm not! It would be fun: a birthday dip!"

They could see far out across the water, which had come right in and gobbled up the beach. Evening bathers bobbed up and down, shrieking and splashing.

"Well, if the evening goes how I reckon it will, someone's definitely ending up in the sea. Maybe even two people. And I'll tell you for free, it's not going to be you or me."

"Ah," said Iona. She raised her eyebrows and then turned her head. "Your Nightshift gals have just arrived."

Harriet and Caitlin-May floated into the Pirate's Paradise. They were number two and three at Nightshift, the publishing house at the centre of town where Rachel worked three days a week.

Harriet Fraser-Campbell was a tall, flawless blonde with long platinum hair and a fixed scarlet smile. Accessorised perfectly, she had a poise that unnerved most people. Rachel idolised her while being nervous whenever she was around. Having her as a boss was intimidating, to say the least.

Harriet effectively ran Nightshift in the owner's absence. She was always meeting people in exotic restaurants and having long lunches with aspiring writers and industry contacts. As for the Nightshift owner, Brenton Tawney, Rachel had only met him once.

It was several months ago, back at the interview. He was a long-haired cadaver of a man with pronounced cheekbones and sunken eyes. Rumour had it he had started life fronting a Goth band called *The Blood.* This made sense to Rachel. Nightshift was an extension of the band. He had moved from music to poetry to fiction and discovered business skills that had established Nightshift as a jewel in the south's publishing crown. Since then, he had been out in the Caribbean, living on some island or other, doing important work and streamlining his tax situation.

Caitlin-May McIlroy was Harriet's number two. Rachel always found her friendly and efficient. She did a lot of the phone work and attended the meetings with Harriet. Caitlin-May had long chestnut hair pulled into a ponytail. She was shy and quiet, preferring to listen rather than talk.

She was glad they had come to her birthday party. It meant a lot. Also, if this Kumi thing pitched up, there would be strength in numbers.

Later on, Rachel's old school friends arrived in a gang. As usual, they kept to themselves and made no effort to speak to her work friends. They just huddled in the corner of the room and gossiped. Rachel thought it was, quite frankly, pathetic. They were just showing everyone what a bunch of losers they were.

When Lake finally arrived later than everyone else, Rachel was feisty.

"Look what the cat dragged in," she slurred.

"Lady, I am the cat." Lake wore a long jet-black shirt, tight jeans, and the boots Rachel liked. His face looked a little roughed up, but he was grinning.

"And who's she then?" said Rachel flatly, looking over Lake's shoulder. The Hello Kitty girl had just waltzed in, several paces behind Lake.

"Beats me. The cat's mother? Happy Birthday, Rach. You'll never guess what I've been doing this week."

"This better be good, or you're a dead man." Rachel turned to Iona for some moral support, but Iona was deep in conversation with Harriet Fraser-Campbell.

CHAPTER 5

Kumiko sidled up to Lake, threw her arms around him, and kissed him.

"Hi Lakie, long time no see!"

Rachel stared.

The girl cast a sidelong glance, said "Happy Birthday" in a sing-song voice, and cut her off to take a drinks order from Lake. Then she skipped to the bar, smiling.

Rachel was dumbfounded.

"I swear I don't know who she is. I've never seen her before in my life," Lake protested. "Listen. Happy Birthday, and I got you this." He handed her a present with a card taped to the top and smiled weakly. "You know how you like those…"

"Lake, you're not getting out of it that easily. This girl says she knows you."

"So what? I know a lot of people – I'm a journalist. Remember?"

"No. Listen. She says you two were 'together.'"

"Sorry, is this a joke because I'm feeling a bit like the punch line?"

"I'll punch-line you. Do you think I'm, like, totally blind, 'Lakie'? I saw the way you looked at her!"

"I was caught off guard," spluttered Lake.

Rachel shot a fierce glare at the bar where little Kumi was buying Lake a drink. Kumi stood up, tossed back her hair, and then blew a kiss toward Rachel. The girl was outrageous. But so was Lake, who had completely failed to be honest and say he was with Rachel. Everything felt like a complete nightmare.

"She's obviously one can short of a six-pack. You know, something's missing up top," he reflected, tapping the side of his head for effect.

"She says she's your fiancée." Rachel was deadpan.

"My what? Nah. Really? I have no clue what you're on about!"

"Lake, I can't believe you'd do this to me. I think you should just go."

"But Rach – this is a mistake! I do not know this girl. I already told you!" Lake exploded. He was suddenly serious; to Rachel, this only proved his guilt.

Kumi was bringing two drinks back to where they were standing. As she approached, Rachel started to feel something inside her begin to crumble. "I don't believe you. I'm out of here," she said, her voice trembling.

She threw out her arm and caught Iona by the sleeve. "We're going."

Iona carried on chatting. "Now," Rachel insisted.

Iona broke off her conversation with Harriet and Caitlin-May, made a quick apology, and followed Rachel out of Pirate's Paradise.

As Rachel scurried to the exit, she tripped over her heels, lurching awkwardly toward the door. Like a true friend, Iona caught her arm, steadying her. Rachel held her head up high again and muttered a parting comment aimed at Lake about him being a complete loser.

"But Rach, I don't know her!" he yelled again.

"I don't know you!" he shouted at the attractive girl, who was dressed in bouquet pink.

"Aww, don't sweat it, mate," said the girl in an Australian accent.

"I was just having some fun. Your girlfriend's a bit highly strung, wouldn't you say? You two must be a barrel of laughs. Anyways, now I've got your attention, I came to bring you a message."

〜 12345 〜

"Where are we going, Rachel?" asked Iona. "Anywhere. I don't care. I just need to get out." "It's your birthday!"

Rachel gulped down a lungful of cool sea air and balled her hands into fists. She felt the sharpness of her nails digging into her palms.

"Did you see the cheek of the girl? She comes to my birthday party – my birthday party – and he just stands there gawping at her." Rachel's heels clip-clopped on the pavement.

"This way, Rachel: the car's over here."

"He's so dead. I mean, who is she? Where did she come from?"

"Australia, I think."

"No, I mean, who is she? Why does she turn up tonight of all nights? And why didn't he ever tell me? After all we've been through? I thought we told each other everything."

"You two are close. I'm sure this is just a misunderstanding."

"We used to be close."

They arrived at the car, which was parked in a bay just off the seafront. "Here, Rach. Get in, and we'll go along the seafront for a while."

"Okay."

Like her house, Iona's yellow 1974 VW Beetle also smelled of sweet tangerines. An air freshener hung from the rearview mirror, shaped like an orange. Iona had attached some colourful crocheted covers to the car seats and customised whatever else she could in a dozen creative ways. Woven floor mats, streamers for decoration, a hippy steering wheel cover. As the throaty engine came to life, ambient dance music pulsed from the speakers.

They set off slowly, moving through the evening traffic. Griffton was busy tonight. A good number of young people thronged outside the seafront bars and clubs along Griffton Boulevard. Bright white shirts and blue jeans. Short denim skirts and bare legs. Laughter.

"Lake and I are… We've been through stuff." Rachel kicked her shoes off into the well at her feet.

Iona smiled, her spiral hair tumbling around her cheeks. She concentrated on the road ahead and let Rachel talk.

"I mean, there are things I've never told you." She turned to stare at Iona.

"I don't expect you to tell me everything."

"No, I mean, we went through some stuff a year ago – when we got together."

"Oh, you mean that horrible man who came into the shop? Yes, I know about that. He gave us all a scare, didn't he? So much so that Ben got the security system. Remember?"

"How could I forget? Yeah, that was part of it. But there's a lot more."

Iona smiled and nodded, wondering exactly what her friend was talking about.

Rachel began to think about her ordeal last year: losing her finger in the night, then the panther attack in the hospital. She recalled the deaths at the Griffton Metropolitan Hotel and her imprisonment in the house on Griffton Cliff. She thought about her vivid dreams of the mountains and the mysterious arrival of Caleb Noble, who had appeared from nowhere and gloriously rescued them. She thought about the Dunamis – a supernatural presence full of power – and Caleb introducing her and Lake personally to him.

There was so much more to life than she had ever imagined. The truth was that she lived her life on the surface. She moved from one thing to another: work to food to sleep, music to books to cafés and bars. She never really plunged into the depths. Last year had given her a glimpse of the vast world beneath and above. Rachel was quiet for a while, lost in her thoughts and memories.

"The problem is I've started to dream about mountains again. I haven't dreamt about them since last year. Huge snowy mountains somewhere in Nepal."

"Mountains?" prompted Iona.

"The thing is, when I dream of mountains, bad things happen."

"I don't get it."

Rachel looked outside the window. "No, I don't suppose I'm making much sense," she mumbled.

⌘ 12345 ⌘

"Okay, start talking," said Lake. He was annoyed that the girl had detonated his relationship with Rachel, although, granted, they were pretty much on the rocks as it was.

"You can call me Kumi."

Lake noticed that, up close, she smelled of flowery perfume. It was surprisingly intoxicating. He thought about Rachel and how he'd been frustrated with her for months. She was either distant or over-the-top emotional: it was one or the other. There didn't seem to be too much in between. It meant they had great times laughing uncontrollably together or sitting quietly, but they also had periods of disagreeing wholeheartedly and shouting at each other.

At other times, she just seemed plain lost, unable to decide what to do about some crisis. She was like an emotional vortex, with all these uncontrollable feelings spinning around. There was Rachel with her big brown eyes, stranded in the middle, trying to figure it all out alone. It made her very attractive to him, though she seemed helpless and solitary.

She needed him, but she pushed him aside. She was a mystery to him, just like that finger of hers. They never found out why it got cut off or who did it.

Lake looked around for a moment and took in the Pirate's Paradise. Rachel's work friends seemed happy to chat with each other. He didn't know them very well, but that suited him fine. As for her old school friends, they just shot him dirty looks from time to time. Lake turned his back to them.

"Kumi, eh? Well, what's this all about then?"

"It was just a bit of fun."

"Bit of fun," he parroted. "You're talking to someone who has a great sense of humour. I can tell you for free that what you did wasn't funny: not at all."

"Suit yourself."

"Though I guess you do have, well, comic timing. I'll give you that."

She smiled and put her hands on her hips.

"What you're going to do now is apologise to all these good people for driving away my girlfriend and wrecking their evening."

Kumi started to chuckle. "You're such a scream!"

"So, what's this message?"

"Ah. The message is, hold on a minute." Kumi extracted a photo from her compact pink Hello Kitty handbag and gave it to Lake. He glanced at it briefly.

"The message is 'hold on a minute'?" asked Lake.

"Don't be a wise guy."

"I can't help what I am."

"Shut your mouth. Look at the picture."

Lake looked properly at the picture. It was a shot of a man in his forties or fifties with thinning grey hair, lines around his eyes, and a stony expression. He wore an expensive suit with a stylish tie and was leaving an office building clutching a tan-coloured leather briefcase.

"Do you know who this is?" she asked. Lake grinned.

"Your dad."

"No, you loser. The message is: 'This is the man who imprisoned you and your girlfriend last year and made her do bad things.'"

Lake felt his hands start to shake. "So what?"

"So what? On the back is his name and office address in the centre of Griffton."

"And what do you want me to do?"

"I'm just going to leave it with you, Lakie. But if you really do love her, I'd do something, and fast."

Lake stared at the picture.

"Listen, it was fun, but, you know, I've got a hot date now: I have to shoot."

"You're going to shoot someone? That doesn't surprise me."

"Jeez, it's just an expression – lighten up!" Kumi gave him a cute smile and kissed him on the cheek.

"You know, if it doesn't work out with Rachel…"

"Get out of here," barked Lake.

❦ 12345 ❦

IONA FILLED in the silence by chatting. She was very good at talking, and Rachel was grateful for it on this occasion. However, as Iona talked, she realised she was unburdening herself about her house situation, which was all news to Rachel. It was probably not what she needed to hear, but Iona had started, so she thought she might as well finish.

The trouble began a couple of weeks ago when a man arrived in a big black Range Rover with tinted windows. He said he represented a property developer interested in buying her house. Being right down on Griffton Boulevard, it really was in a prime location. Iona knew that, and she also knew it would only go up in value.

It was a stunning house, and she loved it dearly. It was definitely the best place she had lived in. Of course, she told the man she didn't want to sell and thanked him for his interest.

A couple of days later, he called her on the phone. Somehow, he had gotten hold of her number, which she was careful not to give out, being a single girl living alone.

He was very persuasive and said his boss would be willing to pay above the market rate, but his offer wouldn't be open for long. Again, she declined and thanked him politely.

Then, last week, the man in the black Range Rover returned to her house after she'd come back from Rock and Shock. This time, he said he was going to give her one last chance to consider the offer, which was the market rate plus fifteen percent. This was a huge amount of money, to be sure. With that, she could probably buy an even bigger place up the road if she wanted. But she still wasn't comfortable about it because she loved the house for its quirkiness, so she said no.

"The man looked pretty unhappy but said he understood my decision," Iona continued.

Rachel nodded.

"But then he said something strange and a bit threatening when he left. He looked at my Beetle and said, 'Nice car. They've got hard shells, but every nut can be cracked.'"

"That is strange," noted Rachel.

Her eyes widened as a large black vehicle barrelled across the divide and crashed into Iona's side of the car. Rachel heard a deafening thunderclap. The VW Beetle lurched violently to the left and came to a grinding stop as Iona slumped over the steering wheel.

CHAPTER 6

One Month Ago

BENSON STEEL GLOWERED as he listened to the weak excuses on the other end of the line.

"You're telling me she doesn't want to move. You're telling me she won't sell. And I'm telling you, everyone has their price. Find out what it is and pay it."

Benson listened to more excuses.

"I don't care how you do it. Buy her out or do something more creative. Just get me that land," he screamed, adding, "Do I have to call the Zodiacs?"

He raised his eyebrows and took one step away from the speakerphone unit on his desk as the person on the phone whined unattractively.

"Excuse me. My time's valuable," bellowed Benson. He paused and said quietly, "Call me when it's done."

He pressed the speakerphone button and sank heavily into his chair. Then he grabbed his hefty metal nutcracker and began smashing a pile of walnuts, shattering the hard shells. He left a scattered mess of broken pieces across the desk, untouched.

Benson was a large man in his fifties with a thick neck and metal-rimmed glasses. He wore a navy blue suit, made snug by his bulk. His office walls were lined with sporting trophies and pictures of him posing with various TV celebrities and high-profile football and rugby teams. He allowed himself one moment to look at the pictures. He rested his eyes on the one of him posing with a top Hollywood actor from a trip he'd made to California.

Then he slammed his hammer fist into the table, making the walnut pieces leap into the air. He jabbed the intercom and ordered up one of his department heads. He planned to terrorise him for the sheer fun of it.

Grinning like a madman, Benson rolled up his sleeves.

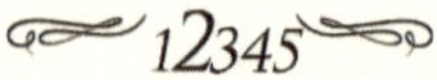

ONE YEAR AGO

BOLIVIA, Central South America.

José Antonio lay in bed after a hot day of farming soybeans on his father's farm. He shared a bedroom with Carlos, Diego, and Sergio, his brothers, who also worked alongside him on the land. He had walked for miles today under the merciless sun and was glad to finally get to his bed. His sisters, Evita and Luisa, had gone to bed sometime before the boys, who wanted to fool and tumble around, tired though they all were.

As he drifted into a powerful sleep that dragged him quickly beneath the surface, he started to dream that dream again. It was the one about the mountains.

He had travelled to the Andes Mountains several times and seen the Bolivian Altiplano in the west, his country's section of the Andes. But these mountains in his dreams seemed different. They were harder and bigger, and the snow blew all the time.

In his mind, he saw the snow and black ice wedged against the steep cliff faces of the mountain. Then he saw a long tear in the mountain, like someone had taken some cloth with both hands and pulled it apart. It was like the mountain was cracking open. It was just like the other year when he had fallen out of a tree onto a rock and cut his leg open. He watched the rip in the mountain grow until it was a doorway that seemed to lead into the very heart of the mountains. Then he saw something else. It was a whirlwind of snow and ice, and it came right out of the doorway.

The powerful spinning vortex lifted away from the doorway and sat outside it, rotating in the air, growing taller by the second.

Suddenly, José Antonio felt a sharp pain in his left hand and let out a cry. He thought the dog had bitten him, and he angrily sat up in his bed to scold him. But he couldn't see the family dog anywhere.

Then he noticed in the half-light that he was bleeding from his left hand. He quickly placed his right hand over the cut and realised his finger was missing.

It was his fourth: the one between his little finger and his middle one.

He cried out again in pain, watching with tears in his eyes as his brothers jumped up in their beds.

Before long, the entire household was awake.

℀ 12345 ℁

JOSÉ'S FATHER and mother woke up quickly and ran to his aid. His younger brother, Diego, had already leapt out of bed. Baseball bat in hand, he was peering out of the window into the yard.

"You okay, brother?" he panted. It was the third time he had asked.

José could not speak. He just sobbed as the pain clawed mercilessly at him.

Sergio and Carlos decided quickly to go outside together to see if they could catch the intruder. One took a torch and the other a poker from the front room fireplace. Their father joined them without a word, his quick brain figuring out what was wrong.

He hugged José, leaving his mother to stay at his side while he hunted down the intruder. Soon, she would apply a cloth to José's wound and a cold flannel to his brow and smother him with anxious kisses.

Meanwhile, Sergio and Carlos hurried towards the front door, following their father, who was now in the lead. He was a strong and determined man with a stern expression and hands like blocks of wood. Fearless, as far as his sons were concerned, he forged ahead, filling them with courage. Diego caught up with his brothers.

On the way out, *Señor* Diez snatched up his shotgun, pausing only to open the door. Diego grinned.

The yard outside was quiet as usual. In fact, it was almost silent except for the breeze ruffling the crops in the fields. The men spread out to assess the perimeter of the grounds. Their father went down the path towards the main road. That was the route any trespasser would be most likely to take if they wanted to flee. However, the moonlit road was empty as far as the eye could see.

He marched to the storehouses, gun in hand.

Sergio wandered round to the back of the house. Carlos traced the circuit the other way, planning to meet him at the back door. They both glanced towards the plains in the distance, though it was dark.

Diego found himself drawn to the tree at the centre of the yard. It was majestic, with broad leafy bundles at the end of each branch. They often climbed it to play in its wide arms. Tonight, however, it seemed like a good place for an intruder to hide.

He squinted upwards. The moonlight and stars illuminated the thick branches of the tree. Then, he saw a bulbous figure sitting near the top. Could it be a two-toed sloth? It looked like a fat, furry monkey with black, beady eyes and a dark, woolly body. He could see it clearly, sitting and staring straight at him.

"Hey, feller," he whispered. "Hey, *Señor* Monkey," he said a little louder.

Moments later, it grew two long, leathery wings and launched its enormous bulk off the branch. The bough sprang upwards, relieved to have lost the extra weight.

With a screech and the flutter of wings, the creature soared into the night air. Diego thought he glimpsed a horrible, bloody, fanged mouth as it gave a last shriek and flew away.

CHAPTER 7

It was going to be a long train ride from London to Glasgow via Edinburgh, but Caleb was in a holiday mood and was pleased to have his best friend with him. The Doctor was a superb travelling companion. He was always relaxed, with an abundance of interesting observations and amusing stories. They had often travelled together, having adventures wherever they went, and this occasion was no different.

They met up at London Euston train station, buzzing with excitement earlier that evening. It was the first time either of them had travelled on the Caledonian Sleeper. So, when Eli Doctorian saw the sixteen-carriage dark blue train with the two pink stripes along the side, he literally clapped his hands for joy and grinned like a little boy.

"There she is! There she is!" he exclaimed.

"It really is generous of you to treat me, brother," said Caleb, not for the first time.

"Don't mention it – every good gift is from above." Eli shrugged. The tanned Armenian was in his seventies, with sparkling eyes steeped in humour and love.

"This is going to be a trip to remember," said Caleb. "And it will be great to see Anton again and spend time hiking in the mountains."

"Like old times," added Eli.

"Yes. Old times." Caleb recalled their travels over the past two decades, the three of them.

Eli had wavy grey hair and a full fisherman's beard: once black and vibrant but now a silver-white.

The Lowland Sleeper set off at ten that night and was due to arrive in Glasgow around eight the following morning. They could smell dinner as they left the busy station and stepped onto the train: vegetables and gravy, slow-cooked beef, and red wine.

Eli turned to Caleb and smiled slyly. "I'm ready for my neeps and tatties. Do you think they have any haggis?"

"Yes, I'm sure they do. And if they don't, we'll request they stop and buy some. Me, I'm looking forward to a glass of Scotch on ice."

⟡ 12345 ⟡

THEY FOUND THEIR SLEEPER CABIN, a compact two-berth room with bunk beds. There was a navy blue, three-step ladder to the top bunk and a couple of orange fabric strips that prevented the sleeper from rolling onto the floor in the middle of the night: a clever design.

Caleb, the younger of the two, opted for the top bunk. The Doctor laid down his bag and sat heavily on his bed. "Ah, this is wonderful, and I am thankful. The Dunamis has led us well." His eyes twinkled as his ivory teeth formed a curved line.

Caleb looked through his complimentary pack of toiletries and smiled. It was made up of a dozen items, including a white towel, a toothbrush and toothpaste, a soap bar, and a razor. There were even cotton wool balls and earbuds.

As an airline pilot, Caleb had stayed in countless hotel rooms across the world and had always been touched by the attention to detail given to toiletry sets. In years past, he made a point of taking home a tiny shampoo bottle, a hairnet, or an extra soap for his wife at the end of his stay. But after Rosemarie's death, he stopped taking the accessories home, and soon after, he retired completely as an airline pilot.

"Toiletries," Eli commented. "You are thinking about Rosy Maria, yes?"

"Did the Dunamis tell you that?"

"No, my dear friend. To me, it is plain. Her friendship was always precious to me, and I admired the way she remained calm each time I brought you back late from another adventure! Come, let us explore our new home. The train will leave soon, and it would be nice to find somewhere comfortable to sit. After all, I am an old man, and I like to sit."

"Lead on, Doctor."

❧ 12345 ❧

THE CALEDONIAN SLEEPER had a series of separate cabins. Travellers had nestled themselves into their rooms, creating a home from home. There were luxurious single sleeper chambers for first-class passengers and standard cabins with single and double bunks. The men walked past several comfortable seats lining both sets of windows, which had their own coffee tables and lamps.

Soon, the train started on its journey to Scotland, and Caleb and Eli settled in the lounge car with some drinks. The carriage had seats arranged around semicircular tables fixed into the floor. A line of glass-fronted pictures hung on the navy blue wall, and an immaculate red carpet lay beneath their feet.

"This is the life," smiled Eli.

They listened to the sound of the train on the tracks and watched the north London suburbs pass by. Houses and streetlights shone into the lounge car. They relaxed and enjoyed being in each other's company.

Then, picking up an earlier conversation, Eli said, "This

matter in the mountains of Nepal reminds me of something, you know. It was during the Forties when all the troops were on the move. It mostly went unnoticed because everybody's eyes were on the war. Of course, the enemy was fully occupied with what was going on there, but some say he was also trying to open the portal at that time."

"Do you think he was close?" asked Caleb.

"Yes, I believe he was. The Protectors found out and stopped him. But Samyaza is a dangerous foe. Only the Rescuer knows what his next move will be. Fortunately, we both know he is a defeated foe, though men may suffer until he is completely destroyed."

⤚ 12345 ⤙

CALEB AND ELI ate a sumptuous meal in the lounge car. Eli didn't get his haggis but settled for a fine, rare steak and vegetables that were lightly cooked. They retold stories from the past of how the Dunamis had led them in testing situations, using them to stage amazing rescues across the world to demonstrate the Creator's love for mankind.

It was during dessert that Caleb indicated with a glance that they were being observed by someone standing behind Eli. Caleb discerned he was a watchman, an agent, and a messenger of Samyaza.

"Behind you. A spy. Table near the door," whispered Caleb with his head down. Eli nodded and continued to eat his chocolate torte, eyes focused on his food. Caleb finished his black coffee. It was a tasty blend, smoky and bitter.

Then, the two men looked up to face the man staring at them.

The watchman was a thin man in white who had experienced too little sun and too much darkness. He had a pencil-line moustache, small eyes, and sweat specked his brow.

"Let's go and talk to him," said Eli.

The two men got up from the table, but the watchman stood up hastily and left the carriage.

"Any leading from the Dunamis?" asked Caleb. "We are to follow him."

"Okay, let's go." They walked briskly to the end of the lounge car, which had eight diners in it. A door led towards the cabins, both first and standard class.

There was no sign of the man in the first carriage, but most of the cabin doors were closed. They kept on walking. Soon, they reached a train carriage with full-length grey-blue sofas on either side. People relaxed, reading newspapers and paperback novels, and paid little attention to Caleb and Eli. They passed some lavatories and another set of sleeper cabins, among which was their own. Before long, they had paced the entire length of the train but seen no sign of the watchman. They paused outside the driver's door.

"I believe he either ducked into a room or hid in the lavatory," said Eli.

Caleb closed his eyes for a moment and listened to the Dunamis. "He is in the lavatory further back down the train."

They turned back and walked past the line of bedrooms. The train wasn't due to stop until it got to Edinburgh and then Glasgow, so there was no escape for the watchman.

As they approached the toilets near the lounge area, they saw him exit a cubicle. He glanced at them furtively and then broke into a panicked stagger in the opposite direction. Caleb and Eli followed, with Caleb leading the way. They were in no real hurry.

They passed through the lounge carriage again, the one with the comfortable sofas. Again, the people paid little heed. But at the last moment, a large gentleman in a tartan green suit and the lady with him both got up from their sofa and blocked the way.

Caleb and Eli waited patiently for the couple to move past them with their bags on their way to their room. Caleb soon lost sight of the watchman, who had taken advantage of the situation to disappear down the back of the train.

Free at last, Caleb and Eli pursued the man, passing through the same cabins as before and into the lounge car. He wasn't in the carriage, so they departed the lounge car and continued to wander down the train. "Good at hiding, aren't they?" commented Eli.

"Yes, but fortunately for us, this isn't the Amazon or the High

Tatra mountains. He can't get far."

They came upon a carriage full of seats but no tables, where travellers snoozed. There was still no sign of the watchman, just holidaymakers and businesspeople with a dozen different reasons for travelling between countries.

At last, they caught up with the watchman. He was outside the guard's carriage. He had been halted by the official and prevented from going into the goods van.

"I wanted to check on my bicycle," stuttered the watchman. "Bicycle, is it? I'm sorry, sir. I don't remember storing any bicycle for you." The burly guard had a thick Scottish accent. He put great emphasis on the word bicycle. "Are you sure it's a bicycle you're after?"

"Oh, it doesn't matter," muttered the watchman. "It doesn't matter anymore," he continued. He spoke in a whiny, nasal voice. The guard shrugged and walked back into his compartment, pulling the door closed.

Forlorn, the pale man turned from the guard and faced his pursuers. His small black eyes darted back and forth.

"Hello, my friend," said Eli.

The watchman recoiled in horror. "I'm no friend of yours," he rasped.

Caleb stepped past Eli in the corridor and stood at the man's other shoulder, pinning him between them.

"Why not let us buy you a drink?" Caleb asked.

"I beg you, followers of the Rescuer and his Dunamis, please don't destroy me," pleaded the watchman. And then he fell silent.

"Come along. Let's see if there is a sofa free in that nice lounge. We can have a quiet talk," Eli said.

❧ 12345 ❧

THE LOUNGE CAR was almost empty now, and several vacant chairs were available. It was midnight, so most passengers had gone to their cabins to sleep. When they awoke in the morning, they would be served a light continental breakfast, arriving at Edinburgh's Waverley Station shortly after.

Eli leaned his highly expressive face close to the thin man's and asked, "What is your name, watchman?" He sat right next to him while Caleb, seated opposite in a single chair, looked on with amusement.

"My name is not important," the watchman replied in hushed tones, his eyes darting around. One of the three other passengers in the carriage quickly decided to call it a night and left without looking back.

Eli stared at the watchman for a while, then smiled. "Your name is Kasimir."

"How did you know that?" snapped the pale man. He became even more agitated, twitching at the shoulders and the wrists.

"We won't harm you, Kasimir. Do you know who we are?"

"You are Doctorian. You are Noble. You are friends of the Dunamis. You are my sworn enemies, and Samyaza will deal with you."

"Good. But tell us, what is your business? And please do not lie, or we will know."

"I cannot speak of that."

"Cannot or will not?" asked Caleb. The man didn't reply.

Eventually, he said, "If I give you a name, will you release me?"

"Okay, watchman. We are reasonable people. What is the name?"

"José Antonio Diez."

"And what about him?"

The man pointed to the fourth finger of his left hand and tapped it lightly. He glanced cautiously at the other people in the lounge and remained silent.

"Where can we find him?"

"I've already told you too much. They would kill me. Now, please let me go," whispered Kasimir.

CHAPTER 8

"Off you go then, my friend," said Eli kindly. Kasimir, the watchman, quickly made himself scarce.

Caleb and Eli got some sleep before their journey to Glasgow and then Jura the next day.

Their friend Anton had lived in the Jura community for the past decade. Neither of them had visited his house on the island, though from what Anton had said, it sounded very picturesque. Surrounded by mountains, the two hundred inhabitants were outnumbered by six thousand red deer on the island. In fact, the island was named Jura after *hjörtr*, the Old Norse word for deer.

Anton had told Caleb once that when he visited Jura, he couldn't move far without bumping into a deer. Caleb had found this amusing.

Anton was an accomplished geologist as well as a keen bird watcher. Being a fan of amazing birds, he had travelled over to see the Snowy Owl spotted on St Kilda several years back. He had even travelled up to Sula Sgeir in the North Atlantic when he heard reports that a Black-browed Albatross was nest-building on the uninhabited island. He was also fond of falcons and had trained as a falconer at one point.

No doubt Anton would be full of bird-related stories when

they finally met up with him. They were looking forward to being reunited, but they still had some journeying ahead of them by road and rail to get to the west coast.

⌒ 12345 ⌒

THE TRAIN RIDE had been enjoyable. But another notable feature of the journey from London to Jura was that Caleb and Eli got to try the direct ferry between the mainland and the island. When it began to operate, it was the first main link to the island in over thirty years, running for just a short period during the year, between April and September. In the past, travellers had always been required to travel to Kennacraig on the mainland, hop over to nearby Islay, and then on to Jura. The trip had taken over three hours in total. In comparison, the new ferry took just fifty minutes.

The boat ride started in Tayvallich, a small village in Knapdale, Argyll, and Bute in the Scottish Highlands. As soon as Eli set eyes on the lovely fishing village, built around a sheltered harbour on Loch Sween, he wanted to stay longer.

The place was a major sailing centre. It had dozens of interesting vessels resting on the water, making Eli quite poetical. But Caleb kept him firmly on track, so they caught the Jura ferry on time.

They boarded the thirty-six-foot rigid inflatable boat, a cheerful blue and white passenger ferry with just enough room for people, bicycles, dogs, and luggage—perfect for the trip. It sped through the water, much to Eli's delight. He opened and closed his mouth and waved his large hands as the boat bounced on the waves. Caleb simply smiled at his friend, eyebrows raised.

Craighouse, on the east coast, was also home to the island's sole distillery, producing Isle of Jura whisky, and the island's only hotel and main shop. Anton lived somewhere in the village. They would find out exactly where when they got there.

As the vessel neared the island, it rewarded the travellers with

49

stunning views of the wild mountain peaks. How Caleb and Eli loved the mountains. They were particularly looking forward to catching the sunset over Beinn an Òir, the Mountain of Gold, and Beinn Shiantaidh, the Holy Mountain. These were the island's highest two Paps, or peaks, which stood at around two and a half thousand feet.

They had also been told to look out for the third Pap, Beinn a' Chaolais, the Mountain of the Sound, which stood southwest of Jura and was the smallest of the three.

"Stunning," said Caleb when he took in the mountains properly. They dominated the landscape of this wild Hebridean island. Grey wispy clouds brushed the summit of the rounded peaks.

"Though my body is tired, this scene is refreshing to the soul and worth the long journey, my friend."

"What a creation," murmured Caleb, taking off his round black sunglasses to take in the true colours.

"Mountains. Always mountains," sang Eli.

"We do seem to be drawn to them. I am constantly reminded that only the one above can create such marvels, not me. They sing of his story."

"History?"

"Yes, that too," smiled Caleb.

"Anton must leap out of bed each morning. I know I would." "That's not bad for a man in his seventies."

"You cheeky young scamp. I'm as fit as a fiddle, don't you know?"

"You certainly are, my friend. But did you know there is somebody buried at Jura who aged even better than you? Up at Kilearnadail cemetery is the grave of Mr MacCrain, who apparently lived to the age of a hundred and eighty."

"Is that so?"

"Well, there was some debate if he really was that old or if he just counted Christmas twice every year."

The energetic ferry quickly drove them from the Tayvallich

pontoons to the Stone Pier in Small Isles Bay. They arrived at Craighouse, the main and only village on the Isle of Jura. Most of the population lived there, with the rest living in tiny settlements along the one main road from the south to the east of the island.

Suddenly, Caleb's face fell as they pulled into the harbour. "Something wrong?" Eli asked.

"I sense enemy activity here," scowled Caleb.

He ran his hand over his closely cropped grey hair and stared into the distance.

As soon as they disembarked from the ferry at Craighouse, they grabbed their bags and set off in search of Anton's place. The first local they met knew Anton, which wasn't surprising given how friendly he was and provided detailed directions. He also mentioned that there was a new standing stone on the island, adding to the several already there, like the one at Tarbert.

"This one has a face, and no one knows how it got there," the man whispered but was gone before they could ask him more.

Anton lived in a neat little white house at the edge of the village. It had four windows on the top floor and four on the ground floor. They immediately noticed the front door was ajar, which was not unusual in Scottish island villages.

In a community like that, everybody knew everybody else and trusted them. Friends frequently popped in unannounced, and the kettle was always on with fresh cakes waiting in the pantry. Doors were left wide open in warm weather, and nobody thought anything of it.

But Caleb and Eli knew in an instant that something was wrong. The house looked unoccupied, and the surrounding homes looked and sounded deserted.

The garden was tidy and pretty, framed by a low wall, and beautiful pale blue and lilac flowers were positioned attractively. Two painted bird tables had been plunged into the grass, one on either side of the path, but there was no food out.

They walked down the narrow stone path, glancing at the windows of the house, seeing brown curtains parted and tied to the side. Nobody was in.

Full of boldness, Caleb strode towards the door and called a "hello" to Anton.

"The Dunamis be with us," said Eli, following Caleb into the house.

Anton wasn't in the front room, the kitchen, or the bedrooms. They noticed some of his drawers were open, and there were papers on the floor. Also, it looked like some of his furniture was not lined up as neatly as it could be. Instead, they sat at strange angles to the wall, which was undoubtedly not Anton's way.

Back downstairs, they noticed a path leading from the kitchen to a small wooden shed at the end of the back garden. They called down to the shed, but no reply came. Just a strange scratching sound: a clawing and a scraping.

The two men rushed to the end of the garden. Caleb pulled open the shed door.

He saw a black bird in an enormous cage that occupied most of the shed. It was a falcon by the look of it. Falcons were native to Scotland, and Anton was very fond of them. They had no idea he kept one in a cage, though. It was unlike Anton to hold such a noble and free creature in captivity, even though the cage was one of the biggest Caleb had ever seen.

"Ah, the Peregrine Falcon," said Eli. "Swift and agile in attack. Graceful and powerful in flight."

Caleb looked more closely at the gigantic bird with its long, broad, pointed wings and short tail. It was blue-grey with a black moustache, crown, and white face. "It seems rather cruel to keep him caged, don't you think? Not Anton's way at all."

Keeping his eye on the bird, he carefully opened the cage and stood out of the way. Meanwhile, the bird waited patiently, ruffling its feathers and shuffling a little. Then, with a hop and a surprising burst of power, the predator broke free and soared into the sky.

"Much better," said Eli, who realised Caleb was stooping down to pick up something. He had spotted a couple of cigarette ends alongside a brown matchbook. Anton was not a smoker.

"Looks like it's from a hotel in Santa Cruz, Bolivia. Kasimir, the watchman, gave us the name José Antonio Diez. I am confident this is where they've taken Anton. What do you think?"

Eli nodded.

CHAPTER 9

Lake stayed on at the Pirate's Paradise after Rachel had left, and, unfortunately, he'd been drinking, which was never good. He hadn't had much to drink, just the pint of beer Kumiko had bought him and another after that. But it had been enough, both for himself and for Rachel's work friends.

"You know me, I love rollerblading. I take them everywhere. The skates, that is. Do you want to hear my top three wipe-outs? I mean my world's best three spectacular, egg on your face, arms, and legs everywhere wipe-outs?"

"No, not especially," said Harriet Fraser-Campbell expressionlessly.

The tall blonde tried to turn to Caitlin-May and continue an earlier conversation, but Lake boorishly continued. Harriet looked at her elegant designer watch for the fifth time.

"In reverse order, then. Number three, I wiped out during the Greater Griffton Cycle Race a couple of years back. I was going top speed when I collided with three cyclists coming down the hill and two who had just stopped for a rest. Absolute carnage! Number two has got to be skating in New York traffic. I was going downtown from Times Square in rush hour when bang! There I am, heading for the underside of a taxi, with people screaming everywhere. Obviously, I didn't die."

Lake grinned, but Harriet looked particularly hostile, and Caitlin-May looked bemused.

"So that's numbers three and two for you. Are you ready for my top wipe-out? Well, number one was down on Griffton Beach. I was trying to impress a girl, you know how it is?"

Harriet suddenly looked stern, so Lake decided he needed to turn up the charm to keep her attention.

"Anyway, she wasn't worth it. She's nothing compared to you ladies. Believe me. Or Rachel, of course."

"Or that little girl you were with earlier?" asked Harriet.

"So anyway, I zoom up to her, doing these amazing crossovers. Then, I suddenly got it into my head to hop a bench and do a handrail slide along the beach wall. You can imagine her surprise when I went over the edge, arms and legs every-where." Lake laughed out loud. "I was gone, baby. Ten-foot drop."

"I guess what I'm trying to say is that I have learned that no matter how many times you wipe out in life, you just have to get up and keep skating. And I think this has helped me in my reporting for the Griffton News. Because you might have mashed up knees and a sore backside, but you know…"

"It might be time to get up and get your skates on," said Caitlin-May, not unkindly. She even smiled, although Harriet was scowling and muttering.

"Thank you, Caitlin-May. You're an angel. I think you're right. It is time to call Rachel."

Lake whipped out his mobile phone and wobbled to the door, where it was a little quieter. He speed-dialled her number and waited.

Rachel answered immediately but sounded distant. "Yes?"

"Rach, it's me. It's Lake."

"I think she's hurt. She's not moving," said Rachel in a small voice.

Lake ploughed on. "I'm sorry for being an idiot. Acting like one, I mean. I don't know her, I swear. The girl. Kumiko. But she gave me something. A photograph." Lake stopped.

"Who's not moving?"

"Iona. She's not moving. But she is breathing. It came at us. The black car."

"Hang on. Slow down. Where are you?"

"Down the road. We were going back to her house. Lake, help!"

"Okay, sit tight. I'll call an ambulance. And Rach?"

"Yes?" her weak voice said on the other end of the line.

"I love you."

⤞ 12345 ⤝

BENSON STEEL ENJOYED STUFFING fruit into his industrial blender and mulching it into oblivion.

He had ordered the aquamarine blender over the web, and when it arrived, it looked hungry and violent. The 'high-power crusher-blender' did the job so much faster than the others, and time was money, even downtime.

The thickset man flexed his biceps, then punched the switch that pulped down the large volume of fruit. He had added mango juice and was looking forward to relaxing in a chair with his pint of smoothie.

He thought to himself. *Work is pressurised as ever. Number one, I have to put up with a bunch of amateurs. Number two, I always have to crack heads to get anything done, though that's the fun part. Number three, there is always so much to get done in any twenty-four-hour period.*

Business empires don't build themselves. If anyone thinks they can just coast along and make it big, they're an idiot. Hard graft is what it's all about.

That was how he had done it. He had begun with nothing at all, the third son of a Griffton quarry worker. While still at school, he started off buying and selling anything he could get his hands on, including sports car hubcaps and handheld computer games. After he left school, he did a stint in the Royal Navy, travelling the world, but after that, he decided to go back into business. The things he bought and sold got bigger and more valuable, such as antiques, paintings, and flashy cars.

Once he had made and saved enough money, he started buying property, and that was when his business empire really took off. He now had over a hundred residential and commercial properties in and around Griffton. He also owned buildings and land in Spain, France, and Portugal, though he never had time to visit them.

"Yes, it's all about hard graft. You wake up, hit the computer, hit the phone, grab an apple, and head to work. That's what it was about. If, every so often, you have to hit a line manager or two, well, that's life. Sometimes you have to get physical to get results," mused Benson.

"Then, from the start of play to the final bell, you have to control the agenda. That means lunch on the run because lunch is for wimps. If someone wanted your time, they had to be able to walk and talk. Meetings are ten minutes max. If anyone can't do their job, they are out the door or out the window. That's business."

Benson Steel didn't have any personal friends. He lived to work, and work was his life. That was why he surprised himself by signing up for a yoga class. It was different. And somewhere deep down, he thought it might be somewhere to meet a nice woman. And he was right.

It had been six years since Bridget had walked out on him. Benson and Bridget had met and married young. Their early marriage had been quite good fun. They looked with anticipation toward an exciting future. But, as Benson started to blossom as a businessman, he felt Bridget was quite frankly boring in comparison.

It wasn't her fault, in truth. It was just that she never really understood him, argued Benson. And he was never really interested in kitchenware, home furnishings, or lemon and basil couscous: all these pointless little things she loved so much. So, they drifted apart, and some years back, their marriage just ended.

He never contested the divorce. For him, the reality was that she got in the way of his work. Benson believed he would never have become the person he was if he had stayed with her. Besides, he was certain that in her heart of hearts, she knew he was too good for her.

The yoga classes had been something of an eye-opener for him because he had always been an outdoors kind of guy. He favoured activity holidays as a way to relax: rock climbing, abseiling, jumping out of planes, that sort of thing.

He always thought yoga was for girls, pregnant mothers in particular, but when he saw the poster down at his gym advertising a new and powerful form of yoga, he decided to give it a try, hooked by the word 'powerful.' After all, Benson Steel was not afraid of anything. That included wearing a leotard if he had to. If anyone tried to laugh at him, well, that would be the last time they laughed at anything.

The physical side of yoga was great for his body. He enjoyed all the stretching and hearing his limbs pop. It was so satisfying. It took time to get over the embarrassment of sitting on the floor with a bunch of girls and a couple of guys, but once he had, he started to enjoy going to the sessions.

Soon, his instructor Janice invited him to experience a more esoteric form of yoga, a transcendental practice that had its roots in ancient Nepalese Himalayan traditions. He made fairly good progress in both the physical and spiritual aspects of the exercises, learning about energy centres and channelling. So much so that Janice singled him out for private tuition, and he enjoyed being recognised.

He didn't feel he had achieved the state of peaceful bliss or ultimate happiness that the exercise promised, as he was still subject to fits of rage, but he carried on anyway. Janice helped him develop his inner side, and he was quickly able to meditate and connect with the spiritual world. But he wanted more than even the highest form of yoga could offer him.

So, Janice helped him to reach further through the discipline of spirit channelling. It was a brave new world and gave him yet another frontier to conquer. Sitting in her front room, in the lotus position, he learned so much.

It wasn't all good, though; sometimes, in his haste to connect, he forgot to use the protective spells, amulets, or incantations Janice taught him to keep the evil spirits at bay. As a result, there were a few occasions when he managed to channel some pretty vile negative spirits. One time, he was doing a random spirit calling and asked an unattached spirit to come through. The result he got was unexpected.

He found himself speaking some sort of spiritual, mixing in the vilest phrases he had ever uttered—and he knew how to swear from his time in the Navy, so that was saying something. Those were very dark times, indeed.

But he eventually found a beautiful astral friend and invited her to stay with him forever. It was about ten months ago that he met the captivating Samyaza.

She always came to him in his mind's eye. She was a beautiful angel of light with long flowing hair and full red lips. She was more delicious than Bridget could ever be. She was his little secret, something no one else could know, not that they would understand.

Samyaza taught him things about the spiritual realms. She showed him visions of towering empires and allowed him to glimpse many powerful and intriguing secrets. Soon, she shared many different ways that he could control the real world and the people around him. He learned about the power of deception and of aggression. She understood his lust for power and success. Bridget had never paid him so much attention or comprehended him so deeply.

He loved Samyaza with a passion. He would happily spend all his non-working time with her if he could. She was wise, funny, and entrancing. And tonight, he was looking forward to enjoying her company. He would sit in his black leather armchair with his vodka smoothie and relax.

Life was good.

⟞⟝ 12345 ⟞⟝

IT WAS the day after the accident. Lake spent his lunch hour perfecting a handrail manoeuvre down some steps in a car park near where he worked. It gave him something else to think about, something other than car crashes, girlfriend troubles, Zodiac beatings, and the man in the photo who was behind the events of last year.

He loved how the metal bar between his wheels slid along the rail and how he needed perfect timing to eject himself and land on the concrete. He had to position his legs and arms just right, keeping everything in balance. The first few times, he took a tumble due to the steep slope, bruising his knee and vowing to wear pads next time. But when he finally nailed it, the satisfaction of mastering the move was immense.

After twenty minutes of practice, he sat on the hard steps and took his lunch out of his backpack. He had bought a beef, mayonnaise, and tomato roll from a sandwich bar near the mall. As he unwrapped it, the aroma immediately made him hungry. He sunk his teeth in. The roll tasted meaty and sweet at the same time, moist with the mayonnaise and tomatoes.

He placed his free hand down on the rough step and thought about his morning in the office. It had been horrible. First of all, he had been late for work. It was partly down to the fact that he was exhausted. He had camped out with the Zodiacs for four days and then turned up late at night for Rachel's birthday, only to face the car accident, the hospital, and all the rest. He had promised Rachel he'd try to see her this lunchtime, but he couldn't face the hospital again when it came down to it. He'd text her instead: check she was okay.

In addition, he had submitted his synopsis for the Zodiacs feature, but his editor, Mike Wright, or as they called him, 'Spike Rewrite' (because he spiked a lot of stories or demanded that they be rewritten), didn't seem to be that impressed.

Spike seemed amenable when he first pitched it. So, on his own initiative, he went undercover with the Zodiacs, well-known in the Griffton community as an uncontrollable menace to society. He found out how they lived and what they got up to, gained some personal insights from gang members, and then got out again.

Spike had loved the idea at the time but seemed far more reticent now, and unfortunately, Lake had argued his case quite hard. "Look, loads of people are going to want to read this. I mean, there's a tonne of really great stuff here. They carry weapons, for one. They're always fighting with each other, so it's not just them against us. There's an angle. I spent a lot of time with these guys, and I got a real sense of the backgrounds of some of them. How society's let them down, maybe, or just how they enjoy doing what they do. There's another couple of angles."

Mike Wright sighed heavily. "I'm sorry. I can't quite see it. You'll have to do better."

"But I went undercover as we agreed for four days. They even beat me up. Tell me it's not that you're scared of them. What, you think they're going to break our windows? What do we pay our security guys for?"

"That's enough Lake. Just do me a favour and run some other angles, will you?"

"It's the shareholders, isn't it? Or the board of directors? 'Risk-averse,' are they? Well, I, for one, am not going to…"

"Just take it easy there. And run some other angles for me, will you?"

"Okay," said Lake, sulkily.

⌘ 12345 ⌘

RACHEL WANDERED across to Iona's ward and stood quietly by her bedside. Iona was asleep. The walk from her own ward had been tough as she checked each sudden noise to make sure there wasn't a panther hiding under a bed. Fortunately, her desire to be with her friend was stronger than her fear of hospitals, or 'hospital-phobia' as Rachel termed it.

"No cats," she informed her slumbering friend. "I bet you don't dream of mountains and monsters and other worlds," Rachel added quietly.

She could hear the rhythmic breathing as Iona rested, recovering from the car accident. Her leg and foot were in a cast and elevated. Rachel stared at her, her mind swirling with dark thoughts.

"Sweet dreams," she told the sleeping Iona. Rachel was dying to be discharged, but for the time being, they wanted to keep both of them in for a bit longer. "I'll check on you again in the morning if they let me," she said.

Before she left her side, Rachel searched the ward thoroughly with her eyes for hidden felines.

⌘ 12345 ⌘

"HOW LONG HAVE we known each other?" said Samyaza soothingly.

"Oh, a couple of months. But it seems like I've known you forever," crooned Benson.

"Well, I've been watching you for a long time, Benson."

"Really?" he growled.

"Yes, wondering if you were the one for me, the one I could work with long term. A partner."

"Oh, I am. You know I am." He looked lustfully at Samyaza, who twisted and turned like mist in his mind's eye. She was provocative, teasing.

"The last man betrayed me so badly. It was so very hurtful. I thought he was perfectly devoted to me. But one day, he just decided to cut me off. After all I'd done for him. He shut me out like a dog, kicked out into the night."

"That's no way to treat a lady," agreed Benson.

"That's right. But I am hoping you are different."

"Oh, I am. I am."

"You have certainly shown me how much you love me by your kind acts of service," said Samyaza.

"You know I'd do anything for you."

"Yes, I know that."

Benson grinned like a child who had been given the biggest ice cream of all.

"But, can I speak plainly?"

"Of course, my love."

"You arranged the accident for the girl, Iona. That was well done. But I really needed you to complete the task."

"I'm sorry. I don't understand."

"You needed to remove the other girl as well. Totally. Out of the picture. That was my desire." She sounded irritated.

"I'm sorry, Sammie. Don't be cross. It was my people: they failed me. But I will deal with it. Don't be stern with me tonight."

"All right, but we may not have long. She is our enemy and could make a choice for the Dunamis at any time. If she does, she may be beyond our reach using conventional means. And I have been patient."

"I don't understand." Benson slurped his smoothie and frowned.

"No, you don't, do you? Well, it would be bad for both of us, let me just say that. It's all in the timing."

"Ah, I see."

"Which reminds me, tonight is the night I said I would reveal myself to you. Lay myself completely bare." Samyaza fluttered her eyelids and smiled flirtatiously.

"Yes, you did mention that." Benson licked his lips and watched the spirit sway her hips and pout.

"Well, now's the time. It's all in the timing."

Benson sat back in his chair and relaxed as he watched Samyaza dance.

Samyaza gyrated for a while but then began to change. She shifted from being a young, attractive raven-haired beauty with flowing tresses and ruby lips into… into what exactly? The luscious locks fell away, and the tall, slender girl shrank and curled up like an old leaf. Her perfect olive skin mouldered and grew pockmarked, taking on a tired, grey hue. Her full lips thinned and darkened, and her large bright eyes dulled and shrivelled into two lumps of hard coal.

"I don't understand," said Benson for the second time. Horrified, he stared at the hideous creature his love had become.

Samyaza was a disfigured old man with a face full of hatred and contempt. The creature cackled and smiled a nasty grin.

"You should see your face," laughed the fallen angel.

Then he added, "It's time for introductions. Let's start from the beginning. I am an ancient one. One of the Grigori. Some call us the Watchers. We were on the earth long before your kind. Many worship us, and they are right to. So should you. We are the powerful ones. You, on the other hand, are a piece of worm-ridden dog meat. You will do my bidding and achieve my purposes. Otherwise, I will take you apart. And to be honest with you, I am growing sick of you, so that really is an option I'm considering."

Benson Steel sat frozen in his chair. His eyes stared out into space, far into the distance, deep into the abyss of his own soul.

His world unravelled before him, and in his head, a phrase played over and over: *Everything is futile.* He had built up businesses, wealth, and the luxuries of life, and for what — to serve demons? His life had no meaning and no point anymore. He was utterly betrayed by the prince of all lies.

His glass of smoothie lay sideways on the floor by his chair, a pool of liquid running towards the foot of the television.

CHAPTER 10

José Antonio Diez loved kicking his leather football around and particularly enjoyed using his full force. His younger brother didn't stand a chance! José feinted to the right and then powered the ball to the left, making Diego trip and stumble. He gasped as the ball sailed past him at waist height and into the goal, making his older brothers, Carlos and Sergio, laugh out loud.

They were having a great day off work. It was good that Diego could join them after school had finished for the day. They were boys again, all boys together like in the old days.

Diego was always bragging about how great a footballer he was, and he was very good. It was only because he wasn't in the fields working full time like they were, thought the older boys. Anyway, it was good to teach him a lesson now and again: it would make a man of him.

The farming life was tough, and they had to work long days, starting early in the morning. Sometimes, the crops were disappointing, which affected the whole family, but football kept them sane. When they played, they danced and tumbled, sang and shouted. They were free.

Football could match any mood they were in. When they

felt thoughtful, they would dribble and pass the ball to each other. When they felt aggressive, they would thunder around with the ball, shoulder-barging each other to the ground. When they felt competitive, they would play three against one or two against two. Passing the ball between them was a great way to relax, passing fast or slow, high or low. For fun, they would do tricks, flipping the ball up with knees or heads or attempting a somersault kick. Above all, they enjoyed laughing together.

The girls, Evita and Luisa, cared little for football these days. In the past, the six children would all play as a team. They would pitch themselves against other families in their neighbourhood and frequently won. But as the girls grew older, other things held their interest.

Papa never played football these days, José noted. When he was awake, he worked his land, expertly farming soybeans and running the business. When he wasn't working, he ate and snoozed in a chair, a copy of the local paper, El Sol de Santa Cruz, open in his lap.

Bolivia, central South America, wasn't a bad place to live, thought José. Their little village near Pajal, southeast of Santa Cruz, got hot and dry; on occasions, it got rainy. When they were younger and their father was building the business, they didn't have much to eat.

For José and his family, this meant that they sometimes survived on water and sugar until their mother could get hold of corn or rice again. She was an angel who would care for them and often go without food herself. The boys loved her for her devotion and vowed to help the family as soon as they could. They were a strong team.

Now that all four boys could work, including Diego when he wasn't at school, times were better than they used to be. The government was helping, too. Farmers didn't have to grow coca anymore and feed the cocaine drugs market. No, these days, there were subsidies for planting other crops.

The Diez family favoured growing soybeans, though they

used to specialise in corn and wheat some years back. But José's father found an ability to cultivate soybeans, aided by the temperate climate and hot summers, so he could provide for his family and sleep well at night.

Next, it was José's turn in goal. He preferred running around, but everyone had to take turns catching and saving.

Since he lost his finger last year, it wasn't easy to save the ball. Not that it hurt too much. It was more strange when he punched the ball with his left hand. Maybe he'd never fully get used to losing the finger.

He had never worked out for sure what happened that night. He remembered waking rapidly out of a deep sleep. He had been in a lot of pain, and his finger had gone: the second one, if you look at it from the back, though people call it the fourth finger. He thought it was their dog, and, in fact, his sisters still had their suspicions.

But they had never found the finger, and no one had owned up to the theft. They hadn't even found a likely explanation. There was something about a monkey or a bat, according to Diego. But it had been dark, and he hadn't been sure. He had been quite afraid, and this could have clouded his discernment.

So, José had lived through the pain and the nightmares. He also dreams of mountains and being chased by wolves across the plains. Sometimes, they got him; sometimes, he escaped. He would wake up in a cold sweat, clutching the stump of his finger and panting.

It took time to get used to not having a whole hand. Some things were easier to do than others. Combing his hair was fine since he used his right hand, but buttons were more difficult, as they had always required both sets of fingers. He knew of two people in the village who had endured far worse farming acci-dents, and one had lost an entire arm in a machine.

Even so, this was his personal problem, something he had to deal with himself. Sometimes, he had a sense of humour about it. More and more, he brooded about it. When he was in one of those moods, it was hard to snap out of it. He knew he was changing.

His family remained superstitious about the whole incident, believing that particular night, the spirits were out.

Then, a couple of weeks ago, something else happened they couldn't explain.

It was the mysterious arrival.

José and Diego had been wandering along the outskirts of the village two Sundays ago. Being the youngest boys, they had always spent time together.

José had only recently finished at the schoolhouse and joined his brothers full-time at the farm. He had missed sitting in lessons with Diego, who was his best friend and his younger brother.

On this sunny Sunday mid-afternoon, they set off to hike out of their village and up to the nearby hills. Like Santa Cruz and the outlying areas, their village was at one of the lowest points in Bolivia. It was set in a vast plain south of the Amazon Basin. But despite this, it was still several hundred meters above sea level.

So, although temperatures frequently rose above what was comfortable, the icy winds from the south, the Sureños, could rise up quickly. They suddenly made their presence felt during May and June, arriving like an unexpected guest from Argentina.

Mama always insisted that her girls and younger boys had some warm clothes by them in case the winds came. They didn't complain anymore because they knew how cold it could get. She had also packed their bag with water and canapé, a kind of chewy cookie made from manioc flour and cheese. And so they were all set for their journey.

José and Diego walked along the dirt track for some time through their father's soybean fields. Unharvested crops fluttered in the breeze, and an Amazonian forest of mustard-coloured tendrils stretched into the distance. Above was a hazy white sky, milky and dreamy.

After walking and talking for some time, they reached the edge of their village. The farms ended, and the dwellings grew sparser. Just before sundown, they made it to the hills.

The day was making its preparations for the night. The sun was returning home, and darkness was encroaching. It was then that they found the new arrival. The colossal stone head, fully ten feet tall, stared at them on the hill. It had two evil eyes, deep-set and sinister.

José had heard of this sort of thing, ancient stone heads. But seeing one here, out of the blue, was unexpected. For starters, it had not been there the week before. They would have known about it.

Second, it looked far too heavy to lift. The whole village would have had to gather to move it, and even then, the Diez family would have heard something.

He knew about the ancient Ponce monolith at Tiwanaku, near La Paz, in Bolivia, high on the Altiplano. That was part of an archaeological site that went back to pre-Inca times. They had called the standing figure there 'El Fraile,' *The Friar*. According to José's father, El Fraile was big and mysterious, with massive stone hands on his stomach. His big, round eyes stared into eternity, but no one could fathom his thoughts.

This was just a head on its own. Made of smooth stone, it had a large brow, boreholes for eyes, a long mouth, and a large jaw. It was set on a very thick neck which rested on the hill.

As José and Diego stared at the head on the hill, they felt it staring back. Diego thought he could hear static, which comes from a radio that is set between stations. It was barely audible, but he detected it.

The younger boy wandered closer to the head, climbing the slope of the low hill. As he approached, José saw the height of the stone head bear down on his brother. Diego was half its size.

"Diego, don't," he found himself calling.

"Look at this thing. I can't wait to tell the others," breathed Diego. "You think they put it here for a joke?"

He carried on walking towards it, his hand rising in front of him.

"Don't," said José, a feeling of dread washing over him.

The structure sat on its own, unaccompanied, on the brow of the hill. It was too far away from the village to be observed directly. They were all alone with the head.

Diego walked around the back.

There was something about the dark eyes of the carving that unnerved José. But, of course, it wasn't alive. He scolded himself for being so stupid.

Diego disappeared for a moment, but it seemed to José like much longer.

When he had completed his full circle, he said, "It's amazing. Must be a practical joke, or maybe some Americans are doing another music video, just like the other year."

He absentmindedly reached up to touch the statue's chin.

The electric current that surged from the stone head sent him convulsing to the ground. José didn't even have time to cry out. Diego rolled downhill and came to a stop at José's feet.

"Diego!" shouted José, his eyes darting between the massive head and his brother's limp body.

⁌ *12345* ⁍

FORTUNATELY, Diego was alive, though temporarily unconscious. By the evening, he was himself again, although the mystery of the stone head remained.

By the morning, word had gotten out, and all the surrounding villages were buzzing with news of the mysterious arrival. There was even talk of the national newspapers and TV stations coming down, though they never did.

That was two weeks ago. Nobody had found an explanation since then, and only the brave and foolish dared touch the stone head.

~ *12345* ~

As his brothers stampeded around, kicking up dust and shoving each other, José spotted their friend Gerardo in the distance. He was running along the dirt track towards them.

Gerardo was one of the sons of the big family that lived down the road. They had just under a hundred hectares of farmland that bordered the Diez property, which grew soybeans, sunflower, and sorghum. It was an impressive business, with three times more land than theirs.

The boy arrived swiftly. He gasped out a handful of words. "Come quickly. The Americans are back. I saw them on the road."

"Man, why us? Why is it always us? Why don't they just leave us alone?" moaned Diego.

The Americans had been troubling the Diez family for many months. They worked for a multinational on the outskirts of Santa Cruz. The brothers were not entirely sure why they came to talk to Papa. Carlos believed they wanted some sort of protection money. They always arrived en masse with guns and dogs. Sergio thought they wanted the farm and the family to leave the village.

Diego was certain the men wanted Papa to return to growing coca, believing they worked for a drug baron. Nobody was really sure why the men came. They didn't dare ask Papa, but it was clear the men spelt bad news. There was always some shouting involved, and sometimes Papa looked roughed up.

It would be a dream come true to get rid of the men once and for all, and perhaps today was the boys' chance, thought Diego with a sudden rush of bravado. Papa would have to deal with his pride later.

"Let's run, boys," shouted Carlos, the eldest. He left the football behind and broke into a trot. Sergio followed.

Soon, the four of them were sprinting full pelt up the track.

Their farm was in the distance, a series of brick outhouses, with their home further up the road.

They passed two smaller storehouses filled with brown sacks and the bottle-green, gasoline-powered tractor they had used the previous day. Next, they approached the large storehouse that held the machinery and tools. Suddenly, they saw a shadowy figure bounding along the path. It was a large shape that was unfamiliar in these parts. It came to a halt in front of them.

"Is that what I think it is?" cried Diego, his eyes widening.

The giant cheetah stared at the boys with red eyes. He licked his whiskery chops.

CHAPTER 11

"Slowly, brothers," Carlos whispered. "If we run, he might come after us."

The boys stared at the beast. José knew from school that cheetahs were the fastest of the big cats. They could run at an average speed of over seventy kilometres per hour. He also remembered they killed their prey by suffocating them, clamping on their windpipe.

"I think this one took your finger," said Diego. "You think?" asked José.

"Definitely."

"He is a monster," agreed José.

Beautiful and sleek, it was the first cheetah they had seen in real life, outside the picture books. He had long, clearly defined features and a golden coat dappled with round black spots.

He lifted his head up and eyed them grimly. "Man, we'd better scram," murmured José.

"I never knew those Americans had big cats like this," said Diego. "I hope Papa and Mama are safe."

"What do we do, Carlos?" said Sergio. "Split up, or stick together?"

Taking control, Carlos looked around them, then asserted,

"José, Diego, you go back slowly to the store. When you get there, close the doors. Sergio, you come this way with me to the machinery shed. Papa has his shotgun there. You load, I'll shoot. We'll see to the cat. You two get something to defend yourselves. Go."

Keeping his eye on the cheetah, José grabbed Diego's hand. He made contact, instantly feeling the absence of his finger: the aching stub where his digit had been severed. Together, they looked at the beast and started to edge backward. José thought that if they were no threat to the cat, he would not attack them. Surely it was the same rule for hornets and wild dogs?

Meanwhile, the older two made their way slowly towards the machinery store to their left. The cat looked at them all suspiciously. First, it gazed at the younger two and then the older two, keeping all of them in sight.

All the while, the only thought that ran through José's mind was, "You can't outrun a cheetah."

❧ 12345 ❧

THE PLAN WORKED, and their manoeuvre confused the animal enough for them to reach their destinations. Carlos and Sergio were in the machinery room hunting for the shotgun. They had stealthily pulled the door closed and were safe for now.

José breathed in the strong smell of soybeans. The aroma was so familiar because he had worked with them forever. But as he panted, it was as though he was inhaling the musty stench for the first time.

Diego shut the door and wedged a chair up against the door just in case the cheetah burst through. José looked around the familiar building with its sacks of harvested soybeans and various long metal tools. The floor was criss-crossed with straw. He grabbed a long wooden pole and swung it around in preparation to take on the cheetah.

Diego grinned, finding humour in the grim situation. "We

should teach that cat a lesson. Are you going to smash him in the face?"

"Yeah. I'm going to smash him on the nose, in the face, whatever."

Diego found a weapon, the wooden baseball bat from last summer. It was battered and worn but felt like a good weight in his hand.

José climbed up on some blocks of wood to peek out of the small window at the top of the storehouse. Papa had put it in for ventilation, and José could see quite a distance through the hole.

He worked out that his brothers were still inside the machinery store. He had a view of the road that led up to their house, which showed two big Jeeps parked near their house up the road. This meant there were probably between four and eight Americans, which was not good news for Papa.

"Diego," hissed José over his shoulder. "I can't see the cat. Maybe he's run off."

"Maybe."

"But I can see the Jeeps outside the house again. We must do something."

"We should run out and surprise them. If we see the cat, you smash him in the face."

"Carlos said we should wait for them to deal with the cat, remember?" said José.

"If the cat has run off, there is no problem." "Okay, I'll have one last look."

José squinted out into the sunlight again. He scanned the horizon, seeing the golden-brown land and bushy green grass. There was no sign of the cheetah.

"I think it's all clear."

With Diego behind him, he slowly pushed the storehouse door open. They stared wide-eyed around them as they came out. José was right. The cat was nowhere to be seen.

"Let's run to the house," said José. "I'll race you."

"I just want to look round the back of the storehouse first, just to be sure." Diego started to tread lightly around the side.

"Diego, be careful." But it was too late.

"He's here," called out Diego suddenly. "Quick José. Back into the barn."

Diego darted past José, and moments later, the two boys were back in the storehouse with the door closed. José climbed up onto the blocks and peered out the window. He saw the cheetah coming into view, its slender body catching the sunlight. Though its face was beautiful and gentle, its powerful jaws and strong, muscular frame told a different story.

The creature looked directly at him, then glanced toward the machinery shed as if deciding which target to attack first.

The cat crouched, preparing to pounce, and then leaped into the air. At the peak of its jump, and José could hardly believe his eyes, he saw it split into two cheetahs.

The second seemed to emerge from the first, like a fish leaping out of the water. He saw a black mist rise from the cats and noticed tiny fireworks sparkling in the dark cloud.

Then the mist dispersed, leaving two big identical cheetahs behind. They landed on the pads of their feet and stared at each other for a long while.

One of them went off towards the machinery store at a trot. The other paused and waited outside the soybean store. The boys were trapped.

José jumped down off the woodpile and grabbed his wooden pole.

"Diego. I need to tell you something, but you're going to think I'm loco."

A BOOMING SHOT shattered the still afternoon air. It was their father's shotgun. It was a powerful and dominating sound that sent José scampering back up to the vantage point of his window. He saw that the door of the machinery store was open a crack. One of his brothers was aiming the dark nozzle of the shotgun outside.

He quickly searched to see whether the cheetah had been hit. It hadn't. Instead, it was running towards the other cheetah at full speed. The other beast drew back as if to pounce. Then, at the last minute, both cats leapt effortlessly into the air.

Then it happened again.

José watched as the cheetahs collided. But rather than repelling each other, as physical objects should, they seemed to merge. It was like pouring one liquid into another. Again, a black mist, crackling with electricity, floated above them. From out of the collision came four felines. Each one of them looked identical to the others. They all had the exact same golden fur with well-defined black spots. Each one had the same intense, fiery crimson eyes.

The four of the cats landed on their paws, each facing a different direction. Then they turned and stared at each other, communicating silently. Three of them turned their heads towards the machinery store. It seemed they had formulated a plan.

"Diego, we're in trouble," said José.

He watched as the three cheetahs loped towards the other building. It was some distance away, but no distance for one of the fastest creatures on earth.

The powerful cheetahs converged on the wooden storehouse where Sergio and Carlos hid. When they were about twenty feet from the door, José saw one of his brothers push open the door wide enough to poke out the nose of the shotgun. He let off a round, shattering the relative quiet.

As the kickback from the gun pushed his brother back into the building, he saw the bullet strike one of the cheetahs.

Instantly, it exploded into a cloud of black gas. Misty tendrils emanated from the big cloud, filled with the same twinkling lights José had seen before. Stunned, José watched the dense fog rise from the ground and dissipate. It reminded him of a picture in his father's newspaper. A group of policemen had thrown canisters of gas at demonstrators to drive them back. But this was different. He had never seen an exploding cheetah in real life, or in fact, an exploding anything much, except for fireworks.

He had been giving Diego a running commentary as things progressed, but the latest turn of events had rendered him speechless. Diego was shifting from foot to foot, frustrated that he wasn't being more useful. He clutched his baseball bat tightly as José continued to stare out of his window with his mouth closed.

Instead of scattering, the cheetahs grouped together and took another run at the storehouse. Even the one outside the soybean store joined them. José quickly caught Diego up on the events.

The big cats ran at the doors as one body. José saw his brothers could not close the doors again. He knew they had to do something.

Before he could say anything, Diego had kicked open the storeroom doors. Brandishing his baseball bat, he started shouting at the cheetahs.

"Hey, big bullies. Hey, pussy cats. You mess with us? You want me to smash you in the face?!"

José saw the nozzle of the shotgun poking out again. His heart leapt with joy.

The second shot put paid to cheetah number two. Like the first one, it disintegrated into a thick black cloud of smoke. Tiny fireworks shimmered inside and then fizzled out.

He heard his brother cock the shotgun, which was a two-cartridge weapon. At the same time, he heard shouting near the house and saw a couple of large men moving out towards their Jeeps. They had checked shirts, and one wore a red bandanna. The men had obviously heard the commotion. The next thing, one of the cheetahs had turned from the machinery store and was charging after Diego.

His brothers had reloaded and fired at the third cheetah, turning it into black smoke like the others. But they were too late to stop the remaining animal from leaping at Diego's chest as he wielded the baseball bat.

One of his wild swings brought the bat against the cheetah's huge body. But it didn't knock the creature off course. Instead, it caused Diego to miss his footing, allowing the monstrous cat to bowl him over.

Diego's eyes widened in horror. He watched helplessly as the cheetah pulled back its black lips into a snarl and sank its teeth into his shoulder, all the way to the bone. Diego roared in excruciating pain, and José feared his little brother was about to be mauled to a bloody pulp.

⌒ *12345* ⌒

Daniel William Harcourt had learned so much from Caleb Noble over the past year. In fact, the two men had become great friends. Caleb had saved him from death in the embrace of the icy sea. Consequently, their comradeship had been built on the firm foundation of Daniel's gratitude.

"Oh, it wasn't me who rescued you," Caleb had insisted. "No, the true Rescuer knew all about it ahead of time. He was the one who told me through the Dunamis. I just happened to be passing when you decided to dive off the boat into the English Channel."

"Well, I had my reasons."

"Yes, that's right."

Caleb was like an older brother to Daniel, and they connected on many levels. Daniel immediately recognised Caleb as an intelligent man, learning later about his years of service as an airline pilot.

Like Daniel, Caleb was no stranger to struggle and pain. He saw in Daniel, a man who had made poor choices and become enslaved to the wrong master. While Daniel was to blame for his bad decisions and feeding his dark appetites, he had faced his past with heart-wrenching tears, confessing everything to Caleb in the presence of the Dunamis, fully contrite, fully remorseful for what he had done.

As Daniel shared his story and brought to light things that had been hidden for so long, it became evident he had hungered for power and riches, only to discover that pursuing them was a trap for the soul. He had wrecked countless lives and, in so doing, had shipwrecked his own.

But Caleb also saw the wonderful potential in Daniel, the husband and family man, the hard-working businessman. He was confident that Daniel would achieve great things now that he had turned from his past misdemeanours and bowed his strong will to the one who was far greater than him. Daniel had made the right choice, Caleb assured him. His words were like a soothing balm, his encouragement producing hope.

One of the things Caleb had explained to Daniel, as he grew in maturity in following the Dunamis, was that the battle they fought was invisible as much as it was visible. Caleb had said, "Our struggle is not against flesh and blood. It's against the rulers, the authorities, and the powers of this dark world and against the spiritual forces of evil in the spiritual realms."

Caleb added, "Most people aren't even aware they are in the battle, and so they slumber, shackled to an enemy who despises them and destroys them at leisure."

In truth, Daniel was more aware than most of this hidden world. He was one of the ones who had sided with the powers of 'this dark world' as a follower of Samyaza. But now, his choices and options were different.

Daniel looked at the cheetah padding about in his mind's eye. The open vision that he was experiencing gave him a gorgeous panorama that presented a farm on a hill surrounded by fields. He could see the beauty of the cheetah, its soft fur and sleek face.

But he could also discern the black, spectral stench that emanated from the being. He felt the presence of evil, tearing through eternity with a deafening scream, searching for some-thing—anything—to devour.

Daniel didn't know where the battle was taking place in the world, but he saw it clearly in the spiritual realm when he closed his eyes and listened to the Dunamis. It was his role to assist a young boy, the Dunamis told him. A boy who was about to be killed by a cheetah.

It was the polar opposite of what he was used to doing in the past. He had been accustomed to listening to Samyaza and carrying out his unspeakable demands without question, destroying rather than protecting. But when he chose to turn his back on the darkness, everything changed. Now, he had the pleasure of taking part in the rescue rather than being an agent of entrapment. No guilt, no shame.

Eyes closed and head bowed, Daniel took in the scene. He saw a dusty farm in an alien land. There was one cheetah, which quickly became four, which was a mystery indeed. But then it was one again, and it was unclear how exactly this was occurring. Was this real or a symbolic vision? He didn't know for sure. The big cat was pacing around the body of a boy who was still alive. That meant there was still time.

Daniel pressed his eyelids together and felt the familiar pres-ence of the Dunamis. "Have mercy on the boy," he murmured. "I implore you."

CHAPTER 12

Diego roared in agony as he saw the cheetah raise its head to take another bite out of him. Meanwhile, José burst out through the doors of the storehouse and raced towards his brother. He had it in mind to kick the cat hard in the gut.

Diego saw blood dripping from his attacker's mouth. It wore a bleak expression except for the glimmer of hunger in its eyes. The beast exuded a ruthless efficiency, and the attack felt terrifyingly inevitable.

The big cat bared its fangs and closed in for the kill, pouncing into the air for this attack. This time, it lunged at Diego's throat. He lay still, paralysed with fear for what seemed like an eternity.

To his amazement, the cheetah froze mid-leap, suspended above him as if defying the laws of physics. Its eyes were locked on the boy, but the creature was motionless. It was denied the kill.

Then the shotgun thundered, and the cheetah exploded inches from his face. A cloud of black smoke filled his vision, and he thought he had entered the point of death. But there was no pain, and he could hear himself panting.

The thick mist showered him with tiny shards of light. They fell about him, crackling and spitting. Eventually, they fizzled out, and the gloomy cloud disintegrated. Diego was left alone on the ground beside the soybean store.

Soon, José was with him. Cradling Diego in his arms, he wept over his brother, putting his hand over the ragged wound in his shoulder.

Seconds later, Sergio and Carlos were by their side. They celebrated together with tears but quietly, aware that danger was still in the air. The incident was like the loss of the finger all over again. There was mystery and anxiety; a brother attacked and wounded, and life was out of control. They knew what they had to do. It was time to go back to the house. Shotgun in hand, Carlos, the oldest brother, stood up with determination on his face, leaving his other two brothers crouched around Diego, who was whimpering.

But just as he rose up, he felt the hard edge of a blade at his throat. The shotgun was whipped out of his hand and thrown aside. The large man with the red bandanna towered over him and sneered.

"Kids," he mocked. He stepped back with a swaggering gait, pulling Carlos along with him, still threatening him with the knife. There was another man coming down the hill, carrying a handgun.

"Everything okay?" the man called out to his comrade. They were Americans.

"I've got everything just about under control, don't you worry."

"Well, I guess we now have one big happy family. Let's take 'em up to the house."

"Get up, boys."

"Where is my father?" demanded Carlos.

The man with the bandanna pointed towards the house. "Your father's just fine. Come with us, and you'll see. We're not here to hurt you."

The boys allowed themselves to be led to their front door, the three brothers supporting the wounded fourth.

"I hope you've got a plan," whispered José.

"Yeah, I've got a plan," retorted Carlos, a little too quickly. José knew he had no plan, and his heart grew heavy.

They found more men inside the house, with his father and mother in the living room. Three men were standing, smoking cigarettes, and two were sitting. There were seven in total and possibly more out back.

José shot Carlos a quizzical look. There was no way they could win this battle. The two big men greeted their gang.

"Look what we found outside," said the bandanna man. Carlos asked him plainly, "So, are you going to shoot us?"

"Oh, there's no need for that today. We were just discussing business with your father," the man seated near their parents said. He was an American in his sixties with a sun-weathered face and a tight white suit. He had an easy manner but a hard expression. José took an instant dislike to him.

"I know who you are," spat Carlos. "You're that drug guy. You're scum."

"Carlos," groaned his father weakly.

"No, it's fine Mr Diez. Your son is correct in understanding that our business is cocaine. But we are not ashamed of that. We operate in a free market. But is he aware of our former arrangement?"

"Papa?" asked Carlos on behalf of all the boys.

Carlos's father looked down, his shoulders slumped.

"Your Papa has decided to reduce his soybean activities and return to coca farming. In return, we will help you out."

"More chemical pesticides," said Sergio. "No, thank you."

José glanced at his mother and saw she had been crying. She was hiding her face in her black hair. His father had sunk into his chair, no longer looking like the master of his own house.

The American spoke briskly, "We could sit here chatting all day, but the deal has been agreed. Ron, why don't you go back there to the kitchen and see if you can find us some drinks to celebrate?"

He added, "John, Carl, I need you guys to go back outside in case any of the villagers decide to come visiting."

The two big men in the chequered shirts looked uncomfortable for a moment but slowly turned to leave the room. Something prevented them from speaking about the cheetah attack.

Just before they left, José called out, "If any of you see my pussycats, make sure to let me know?" The man in the red bandanna flinched.

Seconds later, chaos reigned. Ron, the American, came running in from the kitchen, shouting something wordlessly. He glanced behind him, swatting dramatically with his hand.

Trotting after him was a large and muscular animal, which the boys instantly recognised as another cheetah. It swung its huge shoulders as it came loping into the room. Diego cowered.

Behind the cheetah lumbered two huge men covered in brown and black leather armour. One of them had a red and black sash around his waist and possessed the air of a leader. The warriors' expressions were fierce.

Two more came into the room from the front entrance. They shoved the big Americans roughly back into the room and stood there imposingly.

One of the armed Americans seized the initiative. He took his handgun and pointed it at the cheetah, shooting it from just five feet away. The cheetah didn't have time to blink but exploded in a huge cloud of black gas, showering the room with fireworks. As the mist cleared, one of the warriors snatched the weapon effortlessly from his hand.

"You dared to kill Sengemo." It was one of the warriors who had come from the kitchen. He spoke in a strange, alien accent. "Your debt must be paid."

He drew an impossibly long sword, turned to the American who had shot the cheetah, and claimed his revenge. He returned the sword to its resting place.

José gasped as the American crumpled to the floor.

"We come in peace," said the warrior with the red and black sash. He towered over the Bolivian boys and the remaining Americans, who looked as though their eyes were about to pop out of their heads.

"Peace?" José felt himself asking. "You call what happened to my brother 'peace'?"

The fighter turned towards him and took a long look at his left hand, the one with the missing finger.

Then he said, "Yes, José Antonio Roberto Diez. You have nothing to fear from us. We are here to protect you."

CHAPTER 13

A YEAR AGO

It was the previous year, towards the end of the summer, and Daniel felt like a secret agent. He had a clandestine mission with an objective and a deadline and needed to move stealthily for fear of getting caught.

On reflection, Daniel realised he had always felt like a spy of one sort or another. Working for Samyaza, he was often required to steal, kill, or destroy something or somebody. His business associates all knew him as a manipulative and slick individual. This was even before he had known Samyaza. Then, as he slipped deeper into Samyaza's world, they began to consider him ruthless and brilliant as well. People were in awe of him.

If only they knew the half of it. In private, his thoughts and actions had often been far darker than he had let on. Evil was captivating, particularly during the four years he had worked for Samyaza. The dark angel had taught him about spell casting, shape-shifting, and sorcery, but Daniel found his appetite to be insatiable.

Soon, he was addicted to studying the occult in order to find out more and manipulate more. There was always more knowledge to be gained, more skills to master, and more portals to open.

He led a double life. He was one thing to his family and colleagues. But he was something else to Samyaza and the people who had the misfortune of meeting him when he was on a mission. On one level, he hid his knowledge of the dark arts from his family and friends. On another, he made it known to those from whom he had something to gain or those he sought to control. When it came to the local occultists, they knew him as a powerful overlord. They revered him as someone who had a hotline to Samyaza. They feared him.

But keeping everything secret from his wife, Arabella Samantha, and his boys, Cameron and Rory, tore him apart. He had counted it as part of the cost of following Samyaza. He had rationalised it, though it had torn his very soul.

But one year ago, his life had changed. On rejecting Samyaza and encountering the Dunamis, he had experienced a one-hundred-and-eighty-degree transformation. He had gone from being an enemy of all that was good, with his back turned resolutely against the Creator, to someone who looked to him for strength and guidance, embracing all that was good and true and right. His old life had passed away, and everything was new. Surely, he was free now?

Not exactly: Old habits die hard, and that included his tendency towards secrecy. He still found himself creeping around like a secret agent, as he always had, despite his change in direction. The thing was, he initially felt unable to tell his family the truth, which involved unearthing the shame of the past. And so, he made his amends in secret.

In practice, he found the business of making things right almost as hard as carrying out the crimes in the first place. It was complicated. However, doing the right thing was fulfilling. He was filled with completely new feelings of love, joy, and peace. They welled up within him. But his reputation as a hard man meant he enjoyed these things in private. This was why, one year ago, he was skulking around in the dark in a warehouse in Polcombe, carrying out his secret mission of restoration.

He was conscious that Arabella enjoyed the change in him. That morning, he had come out of his study and given her a kiss. "Do you know something, Bella? I love you. I love you more than coffee." He smiled wryly.

"Oh Daniel, I love you too," she stared into his eyes. Without any warning, she nipped his nose playfully with her lips and then giggled.

He looked at her. She was beautiful. In finding a new life without Samyaza, he had rediscovered his wife. Arabella had her hair in a French plait, with intricate strands of blonde-brown tresses intertwined. One ringlet adorned her playful girl face.

"Let's go away somewhere," she said.

"We could take the kids to Disney World?" "I mean the two of us."

Daniel grinned. "Okay."

⁓ 12345 ⁓

THERE HE WAS, one year ago, standing in Rajesh Patel's cellar. The hair on the back of his neck began to bristle. Daniel was used to hiding in the shadows. But now he was no longer the monster. There was frankly something terrifying about the darkness when he paused to think about it. He had escaped from Samyaza, but he knew Samyaza would not easily forget about him. He knew how Samyaza worked. Demons don't count time the way humans do.

He glanced backwards towards the fire door. It led to the stairwell at the back of the shop.

The cellar itself was bare and functional. An old light bulb cast everything in a yellow hue. Metal shelves supported rows of paper files. An old IBM computer sat heavily on the wooden desk. Odd items of stock were stacked against the yellow walls. Most of the products were upstairs on the shop floor.

Daniel moved towards the safe. He paused again, listening. He wasn't alone.

It was now late evening. He started to hear rustling and creaking above his head; someone was treading carefully across the floor.

Daniel was sure that Raj was out of the country, visiting family in India. There was a wedding going on, and these things often took many days to unfold. Daniel had kept hold of his key to the shop as a form of insurance. However, he had no idea how many other people might have access to a key. Any number of Patel family members could be keeping an eye on the premises.

Then, a thought occurred to him. Had he secured the door when he came in? He had always been meticulous in carrying out his assignments for Samyaza. In the past, he would have locked himself into the building, of course. It kept out prying eyes and unwanted visitors. It also meant your victim couldn't escape if he had the misfortune of being trapped inside with you.

He had definitely heard footsteps. He froze, one hand on the safe dial, the other clutching the top of the leather rucksack. It was packed full of gold jewellery, which he had extorted from Raj Patel several years ago. He had been holding the treasure hostage to maintain his leverage over the poor man. Raj was by no means the only man over whom Daniel held sway.

"I must finish the business," he said to himself.

He meant to act quickly, do what he had to, and then confront any visitors who might be above. It was not the first time he had encountered the unexpected during one of his missions. However, in the past, he would have met any obstacle with focused violence or perhaps a more arcane, magic-based attack. But he was different now and would have to rely on other means.

He snapped the dial backwards and forwards expertly. It clicked obligingly. Thankfully, Raj had not changed the code to the safe. Daniel emitted a low sigh of relief. He grabbed a handful of glittering gold jewellery from the rucksack. Then, a familiar voice arrested him.

"Daniel? What are you doing?"

It was Arabella Samantha Harcourt, his beloved. His wife. It was the woman he had left in the dark for far too long. He slowly turned around and looked at her beautiful, astonished face.

"You followed me?" he said dumbly. After years of deceiving and evading, covering his tracks, and inventing alibis, he never thought he would be the one to be spied upon. What pride.

"It's not what it looks like." Daniel knew he sounded like somebody in a TV drama. It was such a cliché. Then he quickly added, "Did the boys get to sleep okay?"

"They're fine. They're at home with Lucy. She agreed to sit at short notice."

"Oh."

"Oh, Daniel. Another woman, I could understand. But not this. We have everything we need. More than enough. Why steal more?"

Daniel said nothing.

"Is there another woman? Dan? Jewellery for her? Tell me there isn't someone else. Tell me anything."

Then, the Dunamis spoke two things simultaneously, as he often did. He had been silent up until now.

The first was, "I have given you a wife. Honour her. The two of you are one." The other was, "Be open-handed. I cannot sanction deceit."

At the same time, Arabella said, "I need to know, Daniel."

Daniel looked away from her. Then he thrust the gold and jewels back into the safe, brought out a pack of notes from his pocket, and pushed them in, too. He wanted to feel the cost of making amends. Finally, he closed the safe door. He went to the desk and sat down heavily in the chair.

"Okay, I'll tell you everything. I promise. But not here. And I'm not stealing. It's the opposite, believe it or not."

He looked down for several long moments, leaving Arabella with her eyebrows raised. The buttery cellar lighting made the two figures look like actors on a stage.

"What I'm going to tell you will raise as many questions as answers. I've not been a good husband. Not really. And if, after you've heard me, you have to do what you have to do, then I understand. But I just want to tell you one thing. I was dead, but now I'm alive."

He saw the tears in her eyes. They were tears of confusion and betrayal.

"Come on, my darling, let's get out of here."

❧ 12345 ❧

ARABELLA SAMANTHA DE HILL could trace her ancestry back several centuries, with notable names on both sides of the English Channel. She could also track her Scottish heritage to one of the nearly extinct Highland clans, hence Rory and Cameron's distinctly Scottish names.

Born into wealth and influence, her family owned several impressive properties, including Lytescote Manor in Griffton. Arabella was an accomplished horse rider, classical harpist, and letter writer with a strong will that could rival Daniel's when needed. He loved her dearly for all of these qualities.

The shock of her husband's secret life had sent tremors through her very being last year. Yes, there were unanswered questions – many of them. But more importantly, it exposed just how distant she had allowed herself to become. She realised they were not close. Not at all.

Daniel had burrowed himself into the mess he was in, and that was plain to see. Messing about with witchcraft and wizardry was unimaginable. With apparent ease, he had strayed far away from her, and that was hard to take.

She knew there had been times when he wasn't at a particular meeting, as he had shown he would be, or in the office working late. She wasn't a fool. But she knew she was not blameless herself. She had enjoyed the lifestyle and asked no questions. That was the shocking thing.

As he told his story, she listened closely and calculated the years that they had been together: the years they had been apart. Daniel had spent years secretly serving the dreadful Samyaza—willingly, as a young man before they were married and then through their early years while the boys were still babies. But in the last four years or so, he seemed to have broken free from this creature of the night, though she suspected he had still been practicing some of his 'dark arts' during that time.

Then Samyaza returned. Rory was five, Cameron was six and a half, and Arabella was oblivious to her husband's life, immersed as she was in motherhood. But now this Samyaza was gone for good.

"So, it's taken you almost a month to tell me that something major happened to you earlier this summer," said Arabella. They had driven back from Polcombe and were sitting in a bar in Griffton.

"Well, guess what? I already knew. It was the moment you came back from that trip to France. I knew there was something different about you. Your eyes were different. They were softer."

Daniel smiled, remembering.

"And this Caleb who came to visit us recently, he follows this Dunamis too, does he?"

"Yes, he follows the Dunamis. He saved my life, you know."

Arabella was quiet for a long time. She softly drummed her long white fingernails on her glass of Chablis.

It was very late at night. The bar at Darkvale Lodge was quiet, being on the outskirts of town, west of their house. A wide-open window drew a cool breeze down from Griffton Cliff.

When Arabella spoke, her voice was tender. "It's all right, Dan; you can relax. I don't need to know everything you have ever done for this monster, Samyaza." She spat out the name as though she had accidentally taken a fly into her mouth. "I do believe you when you say you've changed and you have a new life now. I can see it."

Daniel smiled.

"But I can't live with you. And I won't share my bed with you."

Daniel looked down at his hands.

"For good?" he asked. His wife was more attractive to him than ever. He marvelled at her clear blue eyes and the slender shape of her jaw. But she was out of bounds now.

Arabella sighed heavily. "We'll see. You can take one of the guest rooms if you like. I'll have Marie-Michelle prepare it for you."

Daniel shrugged in resignation.

Then Arabella said, with a surprising warmth in her voice, "Now take me home, my dear."

❧ 12345 ☙

PRESENT TIME

LAKE SCRUTINISED THE PHOTOGRAPH AGAIN, which he had been carrying around for the past two days. It had become a little dog-eared and dirty. He had dropped it a couple of times and smudged it with fingers that had picked mud from rollerblade wheels.

He could still make out the hard face of Daniel Harcourt. He had been stalking him, watching him entering and leaving the office. Lake stared across the road and matched the man up again to the one in the photograph.

The image showed a shrewd and cautious man leaving an office building, concentration marking his heavy brow. There was something very nasty about Daniel Harcourt, thought Lake. He knew with an iron-clad certainty that he was no good. After all, he was responsible for Rachel winding up in all that trouble last year: bombs and blackmail and jail cells. And rats. Lake hated rats. This man was the mastermind behind it all, as far as he could surmise.

He knew Rachel wouldn't lie to him. At that moment, his poor girl was recovering in hospital, and her best friend was in a critical state after the car accident. He felt his rage rising like mercury in a thermometer.

No, Rachel was true to him. He was the one who always let her down. There was no doubt that Daniel was behind the car crash, too. It all made sense. Now that this Kumi girl had crawled out of the woodwork and given him hard evidence, Lake knew he had to grow up and be a man. Whoever Kumi was working for, her people were onto Daniel, and that was enough for him.

Decisive action was called for. He had followed the businessman from his sleek marble office in central Griffton to this upscale French restaurant in the northern part of the city. But he'd spent enough time ducking into doorways and alleys. It was time to take action.

Lake kicked the toe of his right rollerblade into the ground, ready to race out of the shadows and slam the man against the glass of the restaurant. He took a deep breath and gathered his wits.

Just then, a slender, elegant woman rushed up and threw her long arms around the man. She was beautiful and pale, with striking blue eyes and wavy hair that was swept up into a long ponytail.

She kissed the man on the lips.

Two young boys accompanied her, bouncing around a few feet behind. They were dressed in the uniform of one of Griffton's private schools. It was red and blue with an eagle crest, which meant Eagle Manor Boys' School.

Suddenly, Lake's vision was obscured by a bus.

The vehicle hurtled past, followed by a police van and two

large cars. He gasped as the back draft hit him, leaving him with the bitter-sweet taste of diesel fumes.

When Lake finally regained his view of the restaurant across the road, Daniel and his family had departed. They didn't appear to be in the building. Lake would have been able to see them through the broad windows. No, they were gone, and Griffton had no end of wiggly streets, as Lake well knew. These meandered up and down, left to right, harbouring a hundred boutiques and bars. He turned the photograph over in his hand and rapped it a few times against his left knuckles.

His eyes fell once again on the office address on the reverse side. Lake grinned a ghoulish grin.

"I'll get you next time."

CHAPTER 14

Griffton was sleepy after a long day of frolicking by the sea. Sun- lovers had gorged themselves on the beach. Children had left behind mountainous sandcastles and watery craters. Scraps of litter poked out of the pebbly sand. The air was thick with the stench of salty swell and traffic fumes.

Tireless seagulls squawked and soared. They attempted long sorties deep inland from their haven out at sea. Meanwhile, the relentless roar of the ocean could be heard from the beach to Griffton Cliff. Like an old Etch A Sketch toy, the water would delete everything from the beach at night and deliver a fresh start for the morning.

Weary from a day of making merry mayhem, the Zodiacs reclined on the sand. They had beer. They had kebabs. They had entertainment. Stevie Teeth was wrestling Pig, proving his worth as a top dog. But there was a story behind it. Pig had irritated him that day, and this was his way of publicly disciplining him. The rules were no knives and no ear biting. Apart from that, anything goes.

First of all, Pig got a fist to the side of Stevie's head. It looked like a really juicy one, too. He traded it for a kick in the shin, but the gang leader failed to land his foot properly.

Stevie growled loudly and spat at Pig. Angered by the move, Pig got his head low and charged the smaller man, bringing him down. It looked like the number two had the edge.

With his reputation at stake, Stevie needed to respond fast. He rolled with as much force as he could until he was back on his feet. Pig's stomach made a broad target for his boot. He kicked him with overwhelming force, making the crowd cheer.

Once again, Stevie had secured his role as leader of the pack. Pig lay clutching his middle: roadkill. He might have had a bruised or broken rib, but this was not the leader's concern. He ran at Pig's head, drawing his foot back to deliver a kick. At the last moment, he swung his leg high and brought it down slowly, resting it on Pig's body. Then, with a dramatic pause, he executed a backflip over his defeated foe. Athletic and flashy backflips were his trademark move.

Everyone knew there was no competition—Stevie Teeth was the king. More cans were passed around, and the Zodiacs roared into the evening, smoking and swearing as the sun stained the clouds orange, its tendrils stretching across the sky.

☙ 12345 ❧

RACHEL HAD BEEN TROUBLED by anxious thoughts since the car accident. She was eased slightly by the reassurances from the doctors and nurses that her friend Iona would pull through. Iona had suffered multiple broken bones in the accident, one of which had punctured an internal organ. In the car, the pain had knocked her out, which was why she hadn't been able to rouse her friend.

Rachel had been discharged a couple of days ago, but Iona was still recovering in the hospital, so Rachel went to visit her despite her 'hospital phobia.'

For Rachel, that first day after the accident had been a long marathon of medical checks. In particular, the medics seemed to be concerned about her head. They wanted to keep her in overnight for observations, and so she stayed another night. She had taken a nasty knock to the brow when the cars had collided. She wasn't sure if her head had made contact with the door or the ledge in front of her passenger seat. The result was the same. She had a big bruise and some memory loss.

No one said the words brain damage, but Rachel knew they were all thinking about it. They didn't realise she commonly spent hours crying. For her, this was normal. After all, if you'd been through what she had, you'd do the same, she reasoned.

Fortunately, there hadn't been any panthers in the hospital during her stay or anyone who was after any more of her fingers. The first night had been tense for her, as things like that had a habit of finding her. Panthers, cars, tramps, dancing lights, bombs. They all made a beeline for her. No, it wasn't neurological damage: she was just a magnet for freaks and danger.

That initial night in the hospital, Rachel had wrestled with an overwhelming sense of loss. When she lost her finger last year, she felt she had lost so much more than a digit. She had lost her meaning, her significance. Gone were her mother, her father, her friends, and her very normality. She was an alien, free-floating through the space between planets, utterly alone. She didn't fit anywhere, and there was no place in the world for her. She was lost.

Laid out in the hospital, there was too much time to think. Memories of her mother haunted her. Maryam was her core. How could she have died? Maryam had been a powerhouse of love and care, always singing, always smiling. She had loved her father with a passion. That's why he took it so hard. But her mother was also a mine of secrets. Secret recipes and secret songs. Family secrets, hidden histories, an intricate web of relatives that would make a genealogist's head spin. Everyone was 'cousin' or 'brother'. Rachel wasn't even sure who her grandparents were. There were always elders, but nothing clear-cut. Mystery was always in the background with her mother.

She remembered an elderly couple who had travelled from

Kerala to Heathrow and then down to Griffton. Could they be the grandparents? They were small and brown, even to a little girl. The woman squinted and smiled, speaking no English. She gently swatted invisible flies with her head and gave the young Rachel a handful of rupees and a beautiful lace handkerchief. The man, a white-haired Indian gentleman with delicate spectacles, said, "Pretty girl," and stroked her cheeks. But they were not her grandparents, she discovered later, and it was yet another mystery.

Rachel's thoughts turned from her mother to poor Iona. Everyone who came near Rachel ended up getting hurt: first her mother, then Lara and Lake, and now Iona.

"I'm the problem," she had whispered to the wall beside her.

Then she closed her eyes and, before long, was fast asleep and dreaming. But it wasn't the mountains this time. It was desert plains. It was a dream she had been having with increasing frequency over the past few months.

The muscular young warrior straddled a massive white horse. Both beast and rider had long white hair, though the man was in his prime and not advanced in years as his hair might suggest. Both had blazing eyes like fire. The rider was rugged and powerful. He wore a simple platinum crown from which his hair flowed around his handsome, square-jawed face. Rachel knew he was the Rescuer.

He had a long black tattoo down his thigh. It was in long foreign letters, and the markings were revealed through the slit in his tunic. The robe itself had similar lettering, black on pure white. Light armour completed his ensemble.

An army followed him, riding on white horses and dressed in fine linen, white and clean. They travelled across the sands, talking and laughing as they went.

Then, the Rescuer drew out a huge and ornate broadsword from his scabbard. He held it aloft in the air before him and roared. With their heads down, the rider and his army charged forward together.

❧ *12345* ❧

EDDIE RACE, Rachel's father, stared at the wall with dark-ringed eyes but saw nothing. He was reeling from the conversation he'd just had with the businessman.

They were both around the same age. Maybe the other guy was a little older. Anyway, the businessman, whose name reminded him of an old brand of cigarettes, had come to his house. The cheek of it. What was even more chilling was that the businessman, Benson, was just the puppet, just as Eddie had been a puppet. Samyaza was the real force behind the man.

Doubtless, just like Eddie, Samyaza had come to Benson at a low point in his life. He would have promised the Earth and appeared to be the best friend in the world. Then, he would have discovered the hidden agenda. Losing Maryam was one reason he drank. Finding Samyaza was the reason he had continued.

But this latest revelation had struck him like a hit-and-run. It was like the joyrider who comes out of nowhere, taking your legs out from under you with his stolen car.

"Haven't I done enough for you?" Eddie had cried.

"What? Do you think it was you who took her finger? No, it wasn't you. You were a drunken heap in the corner that night. You let me down. No, I had to choose a different means to accomplish that task. I should have anticipated it," Samyaza said through the body of Benson Steel.

Why Samyaza hadn't appeared to Eddie directly was a mystery. He had always come to him as a foul creature in his mind's eye. Somehow, this was even more eerie. Like he'd actually taken over a whole body. Not just a slice of someone's mind or a sliver of their nightmares. Full on possession.

"But why?" asked Eddie.

"I just wanted to keep you on your toes. You know how things go," snarled Samyaza.

Then he told him about his next assignment. This one wasn't

a difficult one, as assignments went. But neither was it something he'd choose to do himself.

⤳ *12345* ⤲

BACK IN THE OFFICE, Benson was jabbing his keyboard with his podgy fingers. The keys made loud clacking noises as he beat them into submission. He was having to deal with over one hundred emails that had come in since he had been away from the office. It was just a matter of hours, for crying out loud, thought Benson. He hated emails.

There were a couple of dozen emails from logistics and operations. Many related to current deals regarding properties the company was trying to buy or sell. A handful of them were from the lawyers, and the finance team had sent many other documents back and forth. Having to copy him in on everything was just evidence of his workers' incompetence.

Then he clicked on an innocuous email about Employee of the Month. This was the straw that broke the camel's back. It came from human resources and promised some sort of champagne celebration for the winner of the accolade. There would be a whoop-de-doo party with canapés, for goodness' sake. Imagine that. Benson hated human resources with a passion. They were petty, bureaucratic time-wasters.

In fact, he hated all his staff. Celebrating the fact they worked for a living was just wrong. "Isn't that what they were supposed to do? Their jobs? It was just how it worked. You turn up, do your job, and pick up a pay cheque. Why make a song and dance about it? They get paid, don't they? That should be reward enough," he thought.

"Employee of the Month? Employee of the Month? They don't know they're born. I shouldn't have to pay them to work here. They should be paying me," he ranted.

He swung a kick at the PC that hung from a cage below his

executive desk. Unfortunately, the blow fractured the hard drive, and his screen went dead.

Benson folded his bulk toward the ground. He jerked the office computer out of its cage with one hand on either side. It was lighter than he had expected, and the monitor, power cords, and cables popped out easily from the back and lay on the carpet. The monitor cable he had to physically wrench off with supernatural force because of the screws. Then he hurled the machine at the far wall.

It produced an impressive crash of metal and plastic before slumping dead on the floor. It even chipped the paintwork near his door, leaving a black mark. Benson grinned.

Pressing the intercom with his forefinger, he said calmly, "Tell the IT department I need another computer."

THE NEXT DREAM came during Rachel's second sleep at the hospital. The Rescuer was sitting under a tree with his generals, a hardy and loyal band of fighting men. They wore light armour and had long swords at their sides, sheathed in ornate scabbards. Their faces glowed with warmth as they exchanged intimate jibes in good humour. Their mighty horses shuffled peacefully nearby, speaking wordlessly to each other as they were fed and watered. Today, the enemy was far away, and there was time to rest.

The men shared some food and laughed. Meanwhile, the Rescuer, this mighty Warrior King, told tales of old. He was a master storyteller, and he crafted his words so they tumbled about him, rhyming and challenging, entertaining and amusing all who heard. His tales had a particular cadence, a rhythm within a rhythm, which rose to a peak and fell to the depths, with pauses for effect. Rachel was mesmerised.

He waved a hunk of bread in the air, his expression drenched with humour. Next, he accepted a metal goblet of wine from a friend and put it to his lips in a measured fashion. As he spoke, he moved his head slightly and looked squarely at Rachel. He beckoned her forward and smiled. She was sitting just outside the circle of generals, these men of valour and renown, noble warriors of yesteryear. Although Rachel knew she had gate-crashed the party, she also felt welcome and honoured to have won the affection of the leader. She came forward slowly and sat amongst the warriors.

She looked up and noticed the sky behind the leader had a striking violet hue, tinted in places with violent swirls of magenta. It was a wide-open sky that stretched to eternity. Around them were ash-coloured mountains, gigantic mountains as tall as the sea is deep.

The Rescuer offered Rachel his goblet. She reached out to take it, and that was when she woke up.

She breathed in the antiseptic air and felt the hard sheets on her skin. She was still in the hospital.

Then she realised that the girl, Kumiko, was standing by her bed.

Rachel groaned inwardly and slumped her shoulders back into her bed. "Not you," she said, half to herself.

"Listen, I feel bad about before," said Kumi. This time, the slight girl was dressed in amethyst jeans and a bubblegum pink T-shirt. It was still far too cutesy for Rachel's liking.

"I really don't want to be your friend."

Kumi held up her palm and carried on. "It was the paper. They put me up to it. I know Lake from there. It was meant to be a joke. A dare."

"You work with Lake? At the Griffton News?" asked Rachel dubiously. "He never mentioned you."

"Sure. Well, I'm in ad sales, not editorial. Traditionally, we're enemies rather than friends. But I've always got time for Lakie."

Rachel gave her a sarcastic smile.

"Anyways, I heard you were in here, and I wondered how you were."

"You can see for yourself. I've been worse. I've been better.

Why don't you go back to the paper and tell them that? And while you're at it, you can tell Lake to pay me a visit, too."

"Okay, I'll pass on the message to him. You can trust me." Rachel doubted that very much.

"So, do you think you'll be out soon? The guys at the paper want to know. You know what journalists are like."

"Not that it's any of your business: I should be out by lunchtime. Lunchtime tomorrow."

"Well, feel better."

Kumi turned to leave. Before she reached the door, she threw back, "You know, you've got a really cute boyfriend there."

Rachel scowled.

CHAPTER 15

By the time Lake walked into Griffton General Hospital the following day, Rachel had already left. They had given her the all-clear with no concerns for neurological damage. He decided not to hang around and departed quickly.

Rachel was back home with her dad. She was wearing a pale white plaster on her forehead at an angle, and she despised it. Eddie was armed with some surprising new information.

"You're telling me I have an uncle I never knew about? Mum's got a brother, and he's in town?"

"That's what he said on the phone." Eddie breathed heavily and audibly through his nose.

"So how come I've never, like, heard of him?"

"You know Mum's family. She had loads of relatives. It was hard to keep track of them."

"But a brother? A real brother?"

"I vaguely remember she used to talk about him. But you know how rubbish I am at keeping in touch with people. Anyway, your uncle Sandeep will tell you everything when he arrives. He's coming straight from the airport."

"He's coming here? You didn't say he was coming here.

What, did he just call us up out of the blue? I need to change my clothes."

"Off you go then. But be quick. He could be here any minute. He wants to take you out for lunch."

"Are you coming?"

"No. I've got work."

"Okay. But do you think it's okay? Him taking me to lunch? Don't you want to come?"

"I'm sure she used to talk about Uncle Sandeep. She had so many brothers, sisters, and cousins. But they never kept in touch after she, you know. And I wasn't any good at staying in contact with her lot. She was always the friendly one."

"A brother!" Rachel raced off up the stairs to get dressed. Eddie sighed deeply and stood staring into space.

❧ 12345 ❧

JOSÉ AND DIEGO were having great fun swirling their new swords in the air. José's was well-balanced, though he thought Diego's was a little too long for him. Dressed in chocolate-brown leather tunics with cinnamon-colored sashes running from one shoulder to the opposite hip, they felt like real tough guys. Diego felt especially macho with his bandaged shoulder.

Now that the Dream Fighters had arrived, they knew everything was going to be all right. Their rescuers had come, and the family was free from the drug gangs now. The best thing was seeing their father standing tall and proud again.

There were three Dream Fighter warriors: the leader, who wore a red and black sash, and his two muscular comrades. Mercifully, there were no more cheetahs. But if there had been, the boys were sure they would be safe.

The Dream Fighters had got them doing training exercises. They had spent the morning attacking scarecrows in the fields. José had jabbed them in the ribs with his sword while Diego leapt in and cut their heads off. They hadn't laughed so much for ages. Even Sergio and Carlos, who always worked so hard, were getting to have fun. The four of them must have looked an amazing sight. Anyone who tried to attack their village would be in trouble. They were the four musketeers, mean killer dudes.

The girls had enjoyed cooking for the Dream Fighters, these fine and rugged strangers from another land. The men spoke in a strange accent and were courteous on the whole. It was clear they had travelled far. Perhaps they were sent from above to protect them, thought José.

⌒ 12345 ⌒

CALEB WAS on a plane over the Atlantic. Eli was eager to get to South America to search for Anton and would send word as soon as he found anything. Caleb would join him in Santa Cruz after his stop in New York.

He was travelling to New York to meet up with Serena, the prophetess, who had gotten in touch with him through his Californian contact. She wanted to meet him, saying it was urgent. He sensed she had an insight or even a part to play in what was unfolding with Samyaza and the Dream Fighters.

He clearly remembered meeting Serena in Bali last year. She had wavy platinum blonde hair and was wearing a summer dress. They had eaten coconut fish by the turquoise sea. Caleb smiled to himself.

The Dunamis had been silent for some time. But in moments like these, Caleb knew with unwavering certainty that he was in the presence of the Creator, whether he was aware of it or not.

As always, Caleb traveled light, carrying only hand luggage with a couple of simple T-shirts—like the black one he was wearing—a long-sleeved ivy-green shirt, his underwear, and a spare pair of black trousers. Apart from his toiletries and a towel, he had little else for his travels, just the shoes he was in and the sweater and coat in his overhead locker. He depressed the button that reclined his chair and folded his muscular arms in front of his chest.

He loved flying, though he still would have preferred to be in the cockpit, making things happen. Plus, the view was so much more satisfying up front. Closing his eyes, he got a little sleep.

At the airport, he had contacted his people: his community. The group of ex-Hells Angel bikers enjoyed tearing up and down the Californian freeways and loved the Dunamis as they loved their brother Caleb. Whenever he travelled anywhere or faced uncertain situations, he would let them know. He was in close contact with one of them, a dangerous-looking dude who went by the name of Digger. But appearances can be deceptive. Digger, once a devoted follower of Samyaza, had successfully turned away from him and pledged to follow the Rescuer and his Dunamis.

Digger always asked Caleb tough questions about his thoughts and actions to keep him accountable, and Caleb had the liberty to do the same. It helped them both to stay focused, truthful, and effective in their lives.

Of course, Caleb would keep his friend informed about how it was going with Serena, the beautiful prophetess who embodied freedom and grace. After all, he wanted to stay on track with his mission. He must get to Bolivia quickly and meet up with Eli and Anton. There was work to do.

❧ 12345 ❧

"THERE'S someone to see you at reception," said Gabrielle, the editorial assistant. "A female someone," she added.

On the other end of the line, Lake answered, "Oh, that'll be…"

"It's not Rachel," she added quickly. "Or your mother." Gabrielle smiled at him, then turned back to her screen where she was shopping for a new handbag.

"Iona?" thought Lake, but remembered instantly that Rachel's friend was still in the hospital, although it looked like she was going to pull through. "I'll be down," he said.

Kumiko was waiting for him at the reception. She was sitting in a black leather seat next to a coffee table. Kumi cast down the fashion magazine she was looking at and glanced up under long, black lashes as Lake approached.

Showcase issues of the Griffton News towered above her on a nearby wall. They created a patchwork quilt of ink and colour. The Griffton News was known for its high-quality photographs and true-life stories. Lake knew he had a comfortable number of front-page, by-lined articles. He secretly hoped the girl had seen some of them as she waited. He enjoyed being a bit of a 'local celebrity.' He had even found a T-shirt with those words on it. He sometimes wore it at the gym, just for a laugh.

"Ah, the enigmatic Kumi."

"Enigmatic? I like that," she grinned, fixing him with her gaze.

"So, to what do I owe this pleasure?" asked Lake.

"Pleasure, is it?"

"You tell me."

"I was just passing. I wondered if you fancied lunch?" She smiled.

"Look. I followed up on that address you gave me. It's true, he was the man. I'm on top of it. I just..."

"I told you. I don't need to know. I'm just the messenger."

"Who for?" he demanded. Then, added hastily, "I mean for whom?"

Kumi assumed a coy expression. "I don't ask questions. You've got your job. I've got mine. So, how about lunch?"

"Today is not such a great idea. I have deadlines."

"Okay. I'll swing by another time."

Before Lake could say another word, she rose slowly from her chair, advanced seductively toward him, and then walked out of the electric double doors of the Griffton News tower. He got a whiff of the girl's floral perfume and watched her as she moved.

"Okay. Back to work," Lake breathed quietly to himself.

⌁ 12345 ⌁

RACHEL RELAXED when her uncle Sandeep arrived. He was an amiable and slightly overweight dark-brown gentleman in his early fifties. A pair of Ray-Bans nestled into his neat grey hair, sitting up on his head. He wore a nondescript brown suit with a cream shirt and no tie.

He had a big smile for his niece. "Ah, little Rachel," he said as soon as he saw her. He then enveloped her in an embrace that confirmed how far he had travelled and how long it had been since he had seen her.

"You are your mother's daughter, definitely. Definitely, definitely. You have her eyes. Yes indeed." He had a rich, sing-song South Indian accent. It was so much like her mother's.

"I want to know everything about her." Rachel's eyes resembled two white golf balls.

"Okay, let's go. I will tell you. My rental car is outside. At the airport, they told me about an excellent restaurant."

She turned to her dad. Eddie smiled and shrugged and said by way of explanation, "I need to get to work."

Sandeep shook his hand warmly. "As I said before, I am in town for a few days. We get together."

Eddie showed a line of teeth.

⌁ 12345 ⌁

ON THE ROAD to the restaurant, Rachel peppered her uncle with questions as he drove. She wanted to know absolutely everything. What was her mum like as a little girl? Was Rachel really like her? How did he feel when she died? Did he come over to the funeral with the rest of the family? What was it like growing up in Kerala? What did they used to play as kids? Exactly how many brothers and sisters were there? And how many cousins? What brought him to Griffton? Was she the reason?

Some of the questions he answered satisfactorily. Most of them he dodged or just said, "I will tell you. Just wait." She consoled herself, knowing that they would have time at the restaurant.

"Where is the restaurant anyway?" asked Rachel.

"I am staying at a wonderful place. So nice. So grand. The restaurant is there. They say they have magnificent European food. You like?"

Just at that moment, a familiar building loomed into view. "Are you staying at…?" Rachel said breathlessly. Time slowed to a halt.

"Yes, this is where I am staying. The Griffton Metropolitan Hotel. Do you know it, Rachel?" Uncle Sandeep beamed.

Rachel blanched and fell silent.

She hadn't been back to the Griffton Metropolitan Hotel since the bombing last summer. In fact, the very thought of the place made her feel physically sick.

She had avoided the blanket of news stories about it being bombed, rebuilt, renovated, and reopened. She had shunned the memorial coverage following the deaths that her actions had helped to cause. It had been in the papers and on the local news for literally weeks on end. Details about the hotel bombing always held a dreamlike quality for her. In the bubble in which she lived, the Griffton Metropolitan Hotel and the incident with the bag had almost ceased to exist. Until now.

Walking through the hotel foyer was a surreal experience. They had embedded a golden plaque on the entrance floor. It resembled a Hollywood star but commemorated the victims instead. Rachel didn't enjoy crossing the floor. There seemed to be too many flower arrangements. There were blooms on tables, vases in the alcoves, and bouquets surrounding a memorial alcove. Rachel felt unwell.

She enjoyed it even less when her uncle led her into the restaurant where she had been instructed to leave the bomb. Agitated, she eyed each hotel staff member as she passed them. Perhaps she looked familiar to them. Would they remember her and call the police?

"Through here," said Uncle Sandeep. In a daze, she floated by his side and found herself in the restaurant. The aroma was of garlic and onions and char-grilled steak.

They didn't stop but continued towards a private dining area towards the back. The room had its own door. She saw a table that could comfortably seat around eight people. A figure sat at the table toward the back of the small room. He was a thickset man in a suit and tie, wearing metal glasses that seemed too small for his head, which bulged out around them.

"I don't understand." Uncle Sandeep closed the door behind her, and she found herself in the private dining room, along with two strangers.

She turned to look at her uncle. "You're not my uncle, are you?"

He smiled and left, closing the door behind him.

CHAPTER 16

Caleb had found a remarkable burrito bar just off Times Square. He had asked for a recommendation from a shop assistant at the M&M's World store in Times Square, who directed him there.

The restaurant made excellent use of the chipotle, a smoke-dried jalapeno pepper favoured by Mexican and Tex-Mex cuisine. This amazing eatery used it to great effect in its gourmet burritos, which featured a mouth-watering hot sauce. Caleb stood and marvelled as he queued at the counter.

Before him was an impressive array of colours: red, green, brown, black, and yellow. The ingredients were housed and displayed in separate metal dishes, some hot and some cold, and the aroma that rose from them made his mouth water. There were dishes of slow-cooked, shredded pork, beef, and chicken; one for shredded romaine lettuce; another for diced tomatoes; and bowls of guacamole, black and pinto beans, and salsas of varying heat levels.

He went for a ginger ale and a barbacoa fajita burrito filled with braised, shredded beef cooked in fresh garlic, chipotle adobo, toasted cumin, pepper, and oregano. But it didn't stop there. The amazing creation was topped with black beans and cilantro-lime rice, shredded romaine lettuce, salsa, cheese, and sour cream. A serving of crispy corn chips and a pot of lime green guacamole flecked with red onions and jalapenos completed the meal.

"You've got to love New York," said Caleb to his tray of food.

When Caleb finally got to sit down and taste his meal, it was as though the inside of his mouth had exploded. Caleb grinned and grabbed for his ice-cold ginger ale.

⁊⁊ 12345 ⁊⁊

CALEB MET the prophetess under the ever-fluctuating lights of Times Square. A thrill passed through his body. Over their heads, the skyscrapers soared: mirrored mega-structures riddled with flickering ads. Ticker tape share prices rolled past in light as the latest movie and theatre show trailers played high above, teasing the eyes and ears.

At this time of the evening, the thoroughfare was awash with travellers and tourists. Cameras flashed as wanderers posed amidst the traffic flow, unaware of the dangers of jaywalking. Street performers entertained the crowd. Meanwhile, tireless pamphleteers accosted strangers as relentless yellow cabs crawled down the road, bumper to bumper.

She had a violet in her hair: a nice touch, thought Caleb. She pulled the thin grey shawl tighter around her slender shoulders as they walked. In minutes, they were chatting away like old friends.

"Yeah, you know, it's so nice to be back in the States again. It's home, even if it is New York! So anyway, I forgot you knew California. You probably won't have heard of my home town, though. No one has." She flashed a smile at Caleb and regarded him through her large, dark brown eyes.

Caleb smiled quietly, feeling schoolboy-shy.

They made their way to the Marriott Marquis hotel, which overlooked Times Square and rose to thirty-seven stories. Once inside, they travelled up to the eighth-floor lobby. Then they crossed the black marble-tiled floor to the high-speed elevator that would take them up out of sight. The cylindrical cubicles looked like rocket ships and had blue neon circles at their bases. They shot up past tier upon tier of balconied floors. Meeting rooms, restaurants, and bedrooms flew by, and still, they went up.

Serena brushed her hand against Caleb's as she grabbed for the handrail. He kept his gaze pointed forward, enjoying the contact.

The couple disembarked at the top of the hotel. From this height, they had an awesome view down through the hotel. Serena cooed and leaned against a curvy metal grid that protected people from falling. The hotel was as capacious as an airport. It also had the accompanying buzz of chatter and activity. The figures down below were tiny, and the colours merged: creams and blues and greys, hazing into the distance. Meanwhile, lights flashed up and down the inside walls as the high-speed lifts flew.

Caleb didn't want to guess how much it would cost to rent this Penthouse 'JW Suite' at the top of the New York Marriott Marquis —'JW' standing for the founder John Willard Marriott —but he knew that anything was possible for the one who held the world in his hands. In addition to meeting their contact, Caleb was looking forward to witnessing the view over Midtown Manhattan from Times Square. He knew it would be spectacular. It would be just like being on top of a mountain.

He knocked confidently on the door.

❧ 12345 ❧

UP ON GRIFFTON CLIFF, a stone head appeared. The hour was late, and nobody was around. It arrived near the edge of the cliff, somewhere near its midsection, resembling a horn on the nose of a dinosaur. The cliff itself oversaw everything that happened in the city to the south. It was a sentry, marking the years and watching a village become a town and then a small city. It saw how the buildings had grown like moss across the valley. Metal cranes had appeared, hoisting tall skyscrapers up toward the sky. The cliff had watched it all alone.

Now, it had company.

The huge stone head soared ten feet tall. Its stern eyes stared out under a thickset brow. The grey monolith bristled momentarily with supernatural energy. It emitted a thick black vapour encrusted with stars. Then it lay cold and dormant, waiting.

12345

"You are Rachel Race, the only child of Eddie and Maryam Race. And yes, that man isn't your uncle. In fact, he works for me. Take a seat," said Benson Steel.

Rachel's stomach tightened with fear. She felt as if she were shrinking into herself, her heart pounding so loudly she was sure he could hear it. She forced herself to move, each step feeling like she was wading through quicksand.

He drummed his fingers on the table, and everything inside Rachel fought to keep her from screaming her head off at 'uncle' Sandeep's betrayal, which had shattered her hopes of learning more about her mum. She felt devastated and livid. A cold sweat broke out on her forehead, and she had to clench her fists under the table to keep from trembling.

Nevertheless, she sat up straight at the opposite end of the table to the man in the tight-fitting suit, staying on her guard. He wore an expensive-looking red tie and a chunky gold watch. She noticed that two places had been laid. There was one place setting for her with two sets of cutlery and a spoon and fork at the top and one setting for the man. Everything was in its right place: a napkin, a water glass, a wine glass, and so forth. There was a stale, leathery odour in the room. The walls pressed in on her, and the walls felt like they were closing in on her, making it harder to breathe.

Eventually, she choked back her tears and found her voice. "Who are you?"

"Oh, I think you know who I am." "Mister Samyaza?" she asked quietly, her voice trembling despite her efforts to keep it steady.

"I am Samyaza," he said in a deeper voice, his eyes becoming small lumps of coal. "Though this is the body of Benson Steel, businessman and property magnate. Today, I am both Benson Steel and Samyaza. How do you like that?"

Rachel was sure that she did not like it one bit. She frowned deeply, hoping to mask her fear.

"I have taken the liberty to order for both of us. I'm sure you'll like it."

"What do you want from me?"

"We'll come to that in due course."

Just then, the door opened, and a slick waiter brought in the first course. This presented Rachel with a dilemma. She could grab his sleeve and cry for help, bolt for freedom, or stay and do nothing. If they wanted her dead, they would have killed her by now. She had gone through that whole rigmarole last year. But staying in the room could lead her deeper into the dark world that she wanted to avoid.

She looked up at the businessman and was overwhelmed by a sense of curiosity. She needed to know about her finger. She longed to find out why she had been chosen. Above all, something deep inside her yearned for the darkness. It was the sense of the unknown, the electric thrill of danger. Where did this man get his innate power from? What was going on in the mountains? Was it anything to do with the horse riders of her dreams?

The waiter put a dish in front of her and left quickly. On the plate was some sort of terrine with slices of crusty bread. She wasn't hungry. Her stomach felt like it was tied in knots, but she forced herself to keep her gaze steady.

"Don't be fooled. By now, they will have told you that I am the enemy. They might have called me, I don't know, a liar perhaps, or someone who can't be trusted. They may have convinced you my only purpose is to destroy. But you know it's not true."

The man started to eat in a precise way. His table manners were excellent, and he chewed his food an adequate number of times with his mouth closed.

"Delicious. You must try some. Perhaps some wine?"

Rachel waved away the request with a tilt of her head, unable to speak. Her hands fidgeted at the sides of her plate, and she suddenly became aware of the absence of her little finger.

Samyaza noted, "Ah, the finger. Unfortunately, it was necessary. But we won't speak of that now." Rachel pulled her hands into her lap, trying to hide their trembling. The waiter came in again as though he had telepathically received the drinks order. He stepped through the dance of showing the label to Benson, offering the wine to be tasted, and finally pouring a generous measure. Again, Rachel declined.

"You got those men to set off a bomb here," Rachel hissed, her voice barely more than a whisper.

"You forced me to carry it."

"And you did well. Very well indeed." Samyaza clapped Benson's hands together and caused him to smile, but it was an eerie puppet smile.

"You played your part in the struggle, and you did it with boldness and courage. The thing is, in every war there are casualties."

"Like Iona?" said Rachel quietly.

"Yes. But ultimately, this war is about total freedom. It has been fought for a very long time. Centuries. Millennia. But the latest chapter began with the Initiation."

"In the mountains?"

"In the mountains, yes. The Initiation is a beginning of sorts. It set into motion a series of events, a chain reaction if you like."

"Why do you need me then? Why me? And why did you take my finger?" Her voice wavered, and she hated how small she sounded.

"In some ways, that was your initiation into the war. But I have already said we will not speak of that now."

They sat in silence for a while. Rachel's untouched starter was replaced by the main course as the waiter came through. This was a thick, succulent slab of red meat with a juicy red wine sauce and crisp sautéed vegetables. The businessman tucked in. But again, Rachel found herself unable to so much as lift a fork. Her hands shook so much that she feared she might drop it.

Samyaza ate flawlessly and carried on speaking. "I want you to work for me again. But not just as a foot soldier this time. I'd love you to be part of something bigger than yourself. It would amaze you to know the wonderful things that are happening and are about to happen. There is a world much bigger than this one. I know you sense it."

He continued, "You have so much potential, Rachel. You already know this is a world where bad things happen. People suffer. People die. You can't prevent that. You might as well enjoy the ride. Deep down, you know it's true. So, what you need to do now is to choose your side carefully. You see, I am the king of the world, the ruler over all things. So, join me. The world, with everything in it, is mine. I can make things happen. I can start things, and I can end things. So, join me. The power is ours. The advantage is ours. No question about it."

"You also have yourself to think about. I mean, who's really going to look after you? Your mother? She's gone. Your father? I'm afraid not. Friends? Even your boyfriend has eyes for other girls."

"He wouldn't," said Rachel, but her voice faltered. She knew she doubted him. She had already caught him staring at that horrible Kumi thing at the Pirate's Paradise.

"So, consider the options and choose your side carefully. You are a wonderful girl who enjoys adventure. I showed you the beauty of the lights, the intrigue, and excitement of a real mission. Have you ever felt that alive before or since? Be part of something great, Rachel. Work with me. I will show you things that will open up your mind. Amazing things on the earth and in the heavens. Beautiful things unseen by men until now."

"Why me?" asked Rachel, weakly.

"Here's the thing. Your life has a meaning. There's a reason you were born as the person you were born into, the life you have in this present age. There is a plan for you and a future. And it's with us."

Samyaza allowed his words to sink in. "In reality, I can't force you to do anything you don't want to. Not really. You've got free will and can make your own choices."

Rachel glanced up at him, fear and confusion warring within her.

"But what I do know for certain is that you very much enjoyed carrying that bag into this hotel. You loved the power it gave you. For the first time in your life, you were in charge. You had the power to decide if people would live or die. Only you. You had the power to decide if you yourself lived or died. You stared at death itself. That's why I chose you, Rachel. You are independently-minded – totally in control of yourself."

"But I couldn't do it."

"That's irrelevant. We're talking about potential here. You have the power in your hands. Trust in me, and together, we can take on the world. All you need to do is make the right decision, right here and right now, to come and work for me and with me. It will be fun – a real blast! I guarantee you will be smiling like a Cheshire Cat at the end of the day." He sniggered.

A Cheshire Cat. Like the one in Alice in Wonderland, thought Rachel. She sat back and let her mind reel with all that she had heard. Samyaza bided his time, enabling Benson to taste the fine cuisine.

The darkness within her was hungry to find its outlet. The pain of her loss and the weight of her angst made the offer sound wickedly attractive. Everyone loves the darkness, she reflected. Vampires and werewolves, wizards, and witches. Everyone loves the darkness. It was attractive and sexy: the mystery and the power, the pull of the unknown. Samyaza was right. When your natural inclination is toward rage, fear, revenge, self-loathing, rejection, and darkness, why swim against the tide?

And the tide was strong. Sometimes, trying to be good was just hard work. It was much easier to give in to your feelings and sink down to the bottom. The world was bleak and sick and decaying. The world was dying. It was time for a fresh start, one where she could protect herself from the darkness by making it her friend. After all, who was going to rescue her from herself and her black, brooding heart that ate her from the inside? Who could ever love her? She was unlovable.

Just then, an image of a man flashed across her mind. He was the Warrior King with a long black tattoo down his thigh and a broadsword in his hand. The Rescuer. He loved her deeply and profoundly with a supernatural love. And he was racing towards her on a white stallion, a battle cry on his lips and his long white hair flowing in the wind. And he loved her. At his back, the Dunamis howled like a mighty wind. She made her decision.

"No."

"No?" echoed Samyaza in a lower voice.

"No, thank you. I don't think I will join you," she clarified, her voice surprisingly steady. It was an act of defiance, an expression of her free will.

"That's a shame," he answered mildly. "Because it means that I must resort to other methods."

He pulled a smartphone from his pocket. "I'm not going to threaten to take another finger or your hand this time. There's no need for that. I would, however, like you to have a look at this. At the time, it went missing, thanks to me. Anyway, you'll get the picture, I'm sure."

Rachel sat statue-still as she watched the closed-circuit television footage. It unmistakably showed her walking into the Griffton Metropolitan Hotel with the green and gold bag with the bomb in it. Next, it showed her entering the restaurant. It was clearly her. Nobody could contest it. Then it ended. Her mouth went dry.

"You're free to go now."

The body of Benson Steel was thrown back in his chair. The big man blinked a few times. Then he opened his eyes wide, gasping for air.

"Get back to work," barked Benson.

"What?" Rachel was confused.

"What do we pay you for?" he added, looking around the room and blinking.

Rachel scrambled out of the restaurant, her pulse racing. She fled the Griffton Metropolitan like a bullet from a gun.

CHAPTER 17

Rachel spent the next few days watching over her shoulder. She endured several utterly bizarre conversations with her father about the man who had claimed to be her uncle but clearly wasn't.

"I'm sure your mother used to talk about Uncle Sandeep. Or it might have been Uncle Suneel. I can't really remember. She had so many brothers and sisters. But this feller seemed to remember you, didn't he?"

"Dad, he wasn't Mum's brother."

"Then it's a mystery, I suppose," shrugged Eddie. "He just made a mistake. It happens, you know."

"A mistake?"

"How about a cup of tea?"

"Why not," sighed Rachel. She determined not to tell her dad about the real 'Sandeep,' the Griffton Metropolitan, and the demonic possession she had witnessed there. For one, she was still processing it. And second, she knew she couldn't trust her dad any further than she could throw him.

Soon she was sitting on her favourite spot on the sofa, sipping tea and reading the Griffton News. There was a story about a stone head that had appeared on Griffton Cliff. They referred to it as 'the mysterious arrival.' Rachel suddenly sat up straight.

The news story read, "A mysterious stone head was left at the top of Griffton Cliff last night. The mysterious arrival has left citizens puzzled about its meaning or purpose. The stone sculpture features a crudely carved face and appears to be electrified through a hidden source of power. Several members of the public received electric shocks when examining the artefact. Two victims are being treated for burns at Griffton General Hospital."

The story continued, "One of the victims, John Nation from the Old Quarry area, said he was walking his dog at the top of the cliff when he saw the head. "It was taller than me and had these dark eyes looking out to sea. When I touched it, an electric shock threw me down on the grass. Who would make something like that? If it's a practical joke, it isn't funny." Sculpture students at the University, along with local sculptors and artists, denied any involvement in either creating the stone structure or placing it on Griffton Cliff. Police have urged members of the public to come forward with any information regarding the mystery head."

Rachel shivered and cast the newspaper aside on the sofa. She was certain the stone head was linked with Samyaza, Benson, the businessman, the creepy stuff from last year, and the Initiation in the mountains. The problem was that her brain seemed too small to connect it all up or understand what was happening.

She spent a restless hour pacing around the house. Her father left quickly after finishing up his tea. He never really hung around for long, anyway. In her room, Rachel stared at her bookshelf, her clothes, and her pile of papers. She looked at the contents of the kitchen fridge three or four times. She glanced out of the windows on countless occasions and picked up and put down her mobile phone with alarming frequency.

Unable to stand it anymore, Rachel threw her phone, house

keys, and purse into her aquamarine handbag, grabbed a black cardigan, and left the house.

Although she was meant to be off sick, Rachel needed to be back at work. She longed to have mundane tasks to do and people around her. It was time to head for *Nightshift*.

⚇ 12345 ⚇

HARRIET AND CAITLIN-MAY were delighted to see her back in the office, even though they had released her for the rest of the week. It was an offer that still stood if she started to feel unwell. After a slew of concerned questions from them and reassurances from her, her colleagues gently let her know there was a lot of work that needed to be done.

Rachel was happy to fall quickly into step. She enjoyed working alongside Caitlin-May, with whom she shared the main part of the office and who was generally very quiet.

She spent the rest of the morning going through her emails, deleting, replying to, and filing them. Next, she took a dive into her paper filing, extracting folders from her shelves like an automaton. She was feeling better already. Shortly after, she turned to her call sheet and began contacting distributors, business partners, bookshops, and others—handling business that couldn't be done by email.

By lunchtime, Harriet insisted Rachel take a break. In fact, she urged Rachel to take two hours for lunch, which was unheard of. Harriet came out of her office to confirm this, smiled a wide, raspberry-lipstick smile, and then went back to her office, which was along the corridor.

"My dear Rachel," said Caitlin-May, rather uncharacteristically. "We were so worried about you. Honestly. The accident and what happened to you and your friend Iona, as well as your boyfriend and that young lady."

Rachel raised her eyebrows and turned towards Caitlin-May, making her blush.

"It must have been horrible. The whole thing," she concluded. Rachel thought for a moment. *It's just nice to be back at work.* Caitlin-May's concern had touched her heart.

Rachel glanced up at the clock as she always did. The time was twelve-thirty, which meant she had until two-thirty. She put on her cardigan, took her handbag, and went for lunch.

❧ 12345 ❧

THE DOOR of the Penthouse Suite of the New York Marriott Marquis opened fluidly. But little could prepare Caleb or the prophetess Serena for what their eyes were about to behold. Serena gasped.

An unusually tall man opened the door and stood back to regard his guests. His face was kind, and light emanated from his face and body. It made the visitors blink as their eyes adjusted.

"Welcome," he said in a voice that seemed to be made up of several voices. "You have travelled far, both of you and must be tired. There are refreshments for you and a place to rest. I am sure you will find these chambers most relaxing."

The angel of light turned slowly and beckoned for them to follow him. Caleb and Serena walked through into a living area with soft seats. A dining table and chairs graced the end of the long room, and a dark mahogany grand piano lay in the middle. The Penthouse Suite was on two levels, and its windows overlooked the lights and skyscrapers of Downtown Manhattan. They felt a breeze but quickly realised it came from the wings of four strange creatures. The beings rose and fell above their heads. They flew up to the internal balcony, an unusual feature that overlooked the apartment's living area on three sides. After spending a few moments near the ceiling, they floated down again.

The four creatures appeared to be human, but each of them had four faces and four wings. Under their wings, they had human hands with human legs coming straight down from their bodies. Each of the creatures had the face of a human being, a lion, an ox, and an eagle, and fiery sparks shot out between the creatures as they travelled. From time to time, they would stop moving and stare at the visitors. Then, they would be off again as if caught by the wind.

Their host turned to them. "Do not be afraid." He continued to lead them through to a beautifully designed lounge area with two dark blue couches and a chair. The angel sat down gracefully on one sofa, with Caleb on the opposite one and Serena in the comfortable chair. There were drinks and canapés on the table before them, and they were invited to help themselves.

Caleb gazed around the apartment, a glass of iced lemonade in his hand. He spied a huge plasma screen and stereo and the baby grand piano further down the room. Peeking at the level above, he saw a drinks bar and a billiard table.

Then, he took in the amazing panorama of New York City, the city that never sleeps. The angel pointed out famous landmarks and praised the Maker for giving men and women such creativity and industriousness. Although the sky was dark, thousands of coloured lights shone out from office windows, illuminated logos, hoardings, and animated ads. New York was alive.

Caleb turned to Serena to check how she was. Her eyes smiled back at him.

The angel looked at them both without apparent emotion, except for the hint of a smile on his lips.

"So, the Initiation has occurred. But we all know there is nothing on earth or above that happens outside of the Creator's knowledge or his will. With that in mind, I am at liberty to share two things. I have a word of assistance and a word of warning. Then you must make haste, Caleb, and travel south as you intended. However, the woman must take a different path."

His soft, multi-tongued voice continued, "But first, to business. It's time to call on the King."

They stilled their hearts and closed their eyes, feeling the

Dunamis fill the room with his heavy presence as he made the Rescuer known to them.

⌒ 12345 ⌒

SHE WAS PRETTY sure it was him. He was sitting in a café, sipping a cup of coffee or tea. Same face, same thinning hair, same glasses. She wouldn't have forgotten him. Not ever. It was the man from Lupus Street Chemist in Sandy Bottom Cove. She had bumped into him last summer when Samyaza had sent her to pick up the bag and take it to the men at Griffton Cliff. No, she wouldn't forget him in a hurry or the legs of the man lying by the counter, a man who was surely stone-cold dead.

"No one's free," the man had told her, and how true that had been. Samyaza had wrapped her around his little finger, and she had been a slave to him. But what did it mean, seeing this man again, here in Griffton? Of course, he had to live somewhere, but here in a café in Griffton? What was she meant to do? Call the police?

Instead, she called Lake.

"I'm looking at him. The man from last year. From the chemist, you know?"

"Hold on, Rachel. Where are you?"

"It's him. I know it is. He looks the same but different."

"You're not really making much sense, Rach. Are you feeling any better?"

"Yes, I'm feeling better," she snapped. "Hold on. Describe him, would you?"

"A man in a suit. Maybe in his thirties or early forties, I don't know. Blackie-grey hair, thin on top. Sharp nose. It's him. I'd recognise him anywhere." Rachel carried on, glancing at him from the bus stop where she was standing.

"Hang on a second," said Lake, making Rachel wait for several painful moments. "Can you see if he's got a briefcase? A light brown executive kind of thing, with a handle, a strap, and a gold lock?"

"Give me a minute." She took a chance and crept closer to the café where the man was sitting. He was reading a newspaper which was open on his table. Rachel peered in.

"It's by his feet. There's a tan-coloured briefcase by his feet." Rachel bolted away from the café and stood with her back to the brickwork of the adjacent shop.

"His name is Daniel Harcourt," spat Lake through his teeth. "He's the reason I sat in that stinking cell last year. The reason you were forced to do all that stuff. The reason all those people died. And I know where he works."

"It really is him." Rachel found herself unable to say anything else useful.

"Do you think you can get off work early?"

"Why?"

"I can meet you at Rock and Shock at five. I've got news deadlines until four, but I'm free after that."

"Lake, I'm not at Rock and Shock. Today is a *Nightshift* day. You know that."

"Well, okay, I'll meet you there then. Five o'clock."

"And then what?"

But Lake had hung up.

A TEAM of three cleaners entered the vacated penthouse apartment. They were preceded by a long metal trolley. Tiny bottles of shampoo and body wash lined the top, beneath which was a thick forest of essential refills: toilet rolls, bottled water, hairnets, and bin liners. The women chatted to each other casually.

As the trolley rolled forward through the entrance and into the main room with the balcony, its wheels slid through a fine powder.

Gold dust.

There was gold dust over all the surfaces. It covered the top of the baby grand like a thin coating of snow. It lined the tops of the chairs and the tables. A film of gold lay over the wooden floor and the rug.

The three workers stared at the gilded apartment with their mouths open.

A tiny shower of gold dust fluttered through the air, down from above.

12345

RACHEL MANAGED to finish early as Lake had suggested. In reality, Harriet and Caitlin-May hadn't expected Rachel to return to work so quickly. They were more than happy for her to leave half an hour early. Lake met her at the outside doors, talking in hushed tones and being far too dramatic.

"You can talk to me normally. He's not around, you know."

Lake smiled sheepishly. "Yeah, I know. I was just practising for later."

"Okay, what's the plan?"

"We go over to where he works. It's not far from here. He works until about six, and then he drives his Mercedes sports car uptown. That's all I know."

"That's quite a lot. And you know this how?"

"Okay, this is where it gets a little bit complicated."

"So, simplify it for me."

"Do you remember that, err, girl, who was there on your birthday? At the Pirate's Paradise, I mean."

"You don't mean Kumiko, the girl you work with?"

"I don't work with her."

"You don't work with her?"

"No! I told you; I don't know her at all."

"Okay, whatever. So, what about her?" Rachel made her expression unreadable.

"Well, she turned up out of nowhere and gave me this photograph." He handed it to Rachel.

She looked at it for a long time.

"Yup. That's him. So, are we going to kill him?"

"Come again?"

"That was a joke. Not a very funny one, but it was a joke. What are we going to do, really?"

"I'm going to confront him about what he did last year. First, we'll follow him home, and then I'll doorstep him like journalists do. He's in his office until six, so we have just enough time to get over there."

"And then what, Lake?"

"Uptown traffic doesn't move very fast. But I have wheels. My dad let me borrow The Beast. It's over there." Lake gestured to the beaten-up old Nissan Micra.

"We'll follow him to his house."

"This is a terrible plan. How do you know he will go straight home? What if he goes to the gym first? Who's to say he won't go out for dinner somewhere?"

"If he does, then we'll follow him there. And then we'll follow him home."

"What if he works late?" Rachel found it hard to hide her exasperation.

"I'll work something out."

"Okay, but I don't like it."

"Just trust me. I'll think of something. Let's go."

CHAPTER 18

The trip from New York down to Santa Cruz, Bolivia, was far from straightforward. Caleb had determined that this particular trip—the quickest route he could find—would take twenty-four hours of travel, covering just over seven thousand kilometres.

The trip also cost him over two thousand dollars, but there was a reason he had invested well during his life as a pilot, earning good money. He had offered to help Serena with her trip back to Europe, but she had smiled gracefully and said that her generous supporters were faithful in taking care of her. He liked the idea that there were people watching out for Serena, just as there were for him. How he loved his biker friends.

Serena had walked with him to the security gate. She held both of his hands as he paused a short distance from the counter.

She glanced shyly at him through her wavy blonde hair and said, "Be careful down there. Listen hard to the Dunamis. I know you will. Go where he takes you. Say what he tells you to. Do what he tells you to do. And I do believe we will meet again soon. I hope we do, anyway." Her voice grew quieter by degrees.

Choking back emotion, Caleb said, "I wish we could have

more time together, Serena. I've enjoyed it more than I can say." At that moment, there was only him and her. There were no other passengers, security staff, airport cleaners, or flight crew. Just the two of them.

"I know," she replied softly.

"Until next time, then, let it be as the Rescuer wills."

"As the Rescuer wills," she echoed. But Caleb feared it would be the last time they would meet.

Their goodbyes were bittersweet, with a lingering hug and tears from Serena. Caleb tried to appear strong but looked deeply into her eyes and shared the moment with her.

Their meeting with the angel had changed them forever, taking them to the edge of their emotions. But then, when the Dunamis had arrived in the hotel room, they were again pushed to their boundaries, utterly undone by the overwhelming love of the Creator for his creatures.

Standing in the airport, Caleb felt both weak and strong: weak as he strove to maintain his composure, but strong as an unspoken passion gripped them both. Deep waters have strong currents that sometimes take you unawares and pull you under, he reflected, like a vortex in the ocean.

And that was how they parted.

❦ 12345 ❦

HE HAD FELT buoyant during his flight from New York's LaGuardia Airport. His mind was filled with Serena and the glorious encounter at the Times Square hotel apartment. His mortal body held the afterglow from the presence of the Dunamis like a luminous star on the nursery ceiling. He felt sure people could see that his face was glowing.

He could still remember every word their host had said. He recalled the graceful movements of the angel and the four creatures that propelled themselves with the power of their wings. They combined the majesty of the big cats with the grace and flight of butterflies. But all the while, they spoke of another kingdom, a supernatural world so different from the physical one he inhabited.

Caleb's mind raced, though he was tired.

At one point, the Dunamis gave him words of encouragement for a stranger. They provided a deep and healing insight into the personal life of one of the Airbus A319's cabin crew. Obedient to the Dunamis, he shared what he was told. It was something about a sibling relationship gone sour. There was deep pain there. But the Rescuer wanted to speak love and hope for the future over the young lady through his Dunamis. She cried.

Caleb saw burdens lifting from the stewardess and a visible change in her demeanour. Deep down, everybody knows there is a Creator who sees every detail of their lives, Caleb reflected. But what they don't realise is how much he loves them. She thanked Caleb profusely, but he humbly told her he was just the messenger. Caleb returned to his seat, having done what he had been asked to do.

The rest of the two-hour trip down to North Carolina, the next stop, was uneventful.

❧ 12345 ❧

BENSON'S FACE was beetroot-red after pumping iron in the gym. Moving on to do his pull-downs, he enjoyed causing a loud crash each time he let go of the metal bar. He also generated distracting grunting noises with every movement and said, "Come on," at the conclusion of every set of exercises. Every so often, someone turned round to look at him, which gave him the opportunity to stare them out until they looked away.

He was dressed in a tight vest and shorts. His chest and back were streaked with acrid sweat. He also sported a red headband that was pressed down to his brow, two inches above his metal glasses. Bits of wet hair fanned out underneath.

With a huge grunt, he released the metal pulley, which sent the black weights smashing into each other like an oversized set of castanets.

"Winning," he shouted. A couple of people left the gym without looking back.

Benson theatrically swept up his water and upended the bottle, glugging deeply. Then he snatched his mobile phone, keyed through his contacts, and made a call. "It's Steel."

"You're going to like this next assignment I've got for you, Stevie baby."

"That's right. You can get the details and everything you need from the usual place. My associate will meet you there tomorrow evening at six. This time, I'm going to need everyone. That's right. The whole gang."

"No, I'll pay you at the end. If there's any of you left. Just joking."

"The usual rate plus a bonus for you."

"Just to give you a flavour, it involves property. And you boys are going to have fun with this one."

❧ 12345 ❧

IN CHARLOTTE, North Carolina, Caleb took another two-hour flight. This one was to Miami. He had an hour to deplane and walk to the next flight, which was plenty.

He was pleased that he was only carrying one piece of luggage, his lightweight pack with his clothes in. It made it easy to nip from one plane to the other without getting caught up in carousel queues. Although he didn't mind waiting and people-watching, queues had the ability to gobble up time.

The next vessel was a Boeing 737-400, a single aisle, narrow-body jet airliner used the world over. In fact, Caleb knew this model made up around a quarter of the worldwide fleet of large commercial jet airliners. He also knew there were roughly one thousand two hundred and fifty 737s in the air at any one time, and that's a lot of metal in the sky.

Of course, he didn't plan on telling anyone any of this unless they asked, apart from Eli. Perhaps he could introduce it into conversation when he met up with him. That would be fun. He grinned to himself, making a couple of passengers nervous.

He hadn't heard from Eli, but this was just as he expected. Eli was from a generation that grew up without mobile phones and instantaneous web communication. He trusted Eli was well and could look after himself, but he had so much he wanted to tell him.

Caleb still had energy, being used to long-haul travel. Sometimes, as an intercontinental pilot, he had been required to stay alert for long hours. Furthermore, his body was used to shifting time zones, as much as the human body can ever really get used to it. As he travelled between Charlotte and Miami, Caleb started to think about his friend Daniel. Daniel's story was remarkable, as was his strength of character.

Towards the end of last year, Caleb helped Daniel and his wife, Arabella, move into their new house. Actually, it was really an old house - an Elizabethan mansion. It was a tragic story that led to the move.

Both Arabella's father and older brother had died last August when the light aircraft in which they were flying crashed. It was unexpected as the craft they used was normally so safe, but it was also unusual because they rarely travelled together. The accident devastated the whole family. Arabella's mother was never the same and moved far away from Griffton, seeking solitude.

Caleb could see Samyaza's hand in it, recognising it as retribution for Daniel's decision to leave his former master and follow the Dunamis. He had seen such things before – a swipe of the tail of the Leviathan, killing and destroying out of pure hatred and anger.

So, during the autumn of last year, the Harcourt family moved into Arabella's family home—a fifteen-bedroom Elizabethan mansion in the northwest of Griffton, just past the cliff. The place was much larger than their previous home, with many rooms, including a billiard room, dining and drawing rooms, and even an orangery. But it needed renovation and repairs.

Regrettably, Caleb was unable to assist with this, though he would have loved to. Caleb had to return to his biker comrades in California and spend some time with them; they were his family, and he had already been away from them for far too long.

But he had kept in contact with Daniel and heard how his massive library and impressive study had been shaping up over time. The boys had particularly enjoyed the billiard room, which they had immediately claimed as their own. Caleb hoped to visit one day soon.

⚮ 12345 ⚮

THE SPARE CAR that belonged to Lake's family was cramped, noisy, and old. It was an ancient rectangular thing that resembled a Lego car. Rachel always hated riding in it.

"Why won't you get yourself a decent motor?" she argued. "Shut up, Rachel, I'm trying to concentrate."

Lake and Rachel had followed Daniel from his office car park. They had skulked around near the entrance, ready to pounce, but initially had a problem starting the Micra. This had darkened Rachel's mood even further. But once they were on the road, they soon caught sight of his dark blue Mercedes sports car and followed him through the slow traffic. They kept their distance, tucked away behind several vehicles.

He drove out of the city centre and traced the roads northwards. Then he went north-west to the outskirts of Griffton.

Rachel tutted and rolled her eyes when she saw that the red petrol gauge light on the dashboard had flicked on.

The traffic moved faster away from town, but Lake's poor car struggled to keep up. Its small engine started to shake and complain as their speed neared seventy miles an hour. A further complication came as the traffic thinned. Daniel's superior machine covered large distances effortlessly. But like a dog being restrained on a leash, he was forced to halt for traffic lights, pedestrian crossings, and slow traffic. This gave them the opportunity to catch up, feeling like the tortoise to Daniel's hare.

❧ 12345 ❧

THE CONNECTION TIME at Miami was even longer, and this was where Caleb really started to feel tired. He had almost nine hours to kill between this flight and the one down to Santa Cruz, Bolivia.

So, at Miami airport, Caleb paid a leisurely visit to a frequent flyer's executive lounge. It was one of the benefits of travelling as often and as far as he did, and the fact he had spent his career in aviation.

Once there, he washed and cleaned his teeth, grabbed some fruit from a bowl in the private lounge area, and chatted with the staff. Then he read a paper and fell into a light sleep, sitting back on a black leather sofa. He still had a night flight ahead of him but was confident he would have the capacity to sleep more on the flight.

Besides, it was going to be a Boeing 757, a mid-sized craft that was quieter and smoother than the other two he had just been on. That should be an enjoyable flight. He might even get some good South American food for dinner. And who knows? They might even have chicken in a Chipotle adobo, though it was unlikely.

As Caleb slid into a comfortable doze, the words of the angel came to mind. "I have a word of assistance and a word of warning," he had said. It was the first angel Caleb had ever spoken to. He had seen angels in the distance and even felt the presence of one in his room whilst spending time in the presence of the Dunamis. The encounter had shifted him into a surreal world where he was now convinced that all things were possible. Caleb stirred on his comfortable couch, his eyelids together.

He brought to mind the rest of the conversation in the penthouse suite.

The word of assistance was about activating the Protectors at the appropriate time. Caleb and Eli knew this was required in order to help counter the extreme levels of activity of the enemy that were yet to come. They were also aware there were three Protectors: one for land, one for sea, and one for air. They didn't yet comprehend what this all meant and would have to be content to wait for direction from the Dunamis in time. Until then, they would have to operate with imperfect understanding and knowledge.

"What I can tell you," said the angel, "is that Serena will know the first location at the appointed time. The Dunamis will tell her, and she will get word to you. As for the warning, the Dunamis says to you, Caleb, 'There are times when silence has the loudest voice. You will not hear me for a time, but when that time comes, do not doubt that I am with you.'"

⤳ 12345 ⤲

EVENTUALLY, the blue sports car was free to fly on the open country roads north-west of Griffton. With very little noise or fuss, it sped up, gliding like a spaceship further into the distance.

"You're going to lose him," scolded Rachel, not for the first time.

"I've been this way before. There aren't many houses up here," Lake replied. "So, it should be easy to see which one he goes to."

"Can you see him?"

"No, but hold on. I reckon I will in a minute."

Thick, verdant countryside hid the road ahead, which snaked left and right, diving between trees and hedges. They climbed around the west side of Griffton Cliff and continued a little farther, passing elms and poplars, then a thicker forest of firs rooted in the light brown, muddy banks.

After a while, Lake saw the sports car a considerable distance up the road, swinging along the arc of a bend and approaching a set of wide and tall wrought-iron gates. He could see the car pause as they automatically opened inwards. On either side of the gates was a towering metal fence that stretched out of sight around the grounds. The fence was made up of thin strips of metal, with unkempt hedges lining the inside and obscuring the house from view.

Lake carried on going as fast as he could and reached the entrance a minute or so after the man had rolled into the drive.

The gates stayed open. Lake slowed to a crawl as he drove close. Both he and Rachel stared into a broad and long driveway that had a massive mansion at the end with half a dozen chimneys and almost two dozen windows facing them. There was no sign of the car.

"I'm going to park outside. You jump out, sneak in, and make sure the gates stay open for me, okay?"

"No, Lake, I want to stay with you. I'm not going in there on my own. Are you crazy? I hate creepy houses."

"I'll just be a second. Go on."

"I could wait outside for you, or we could go in together?"

"No. You need to be on the inside if the gates close. There must be a way of opening them again, or a little door for the postman or something? Anyway, I'm sure they'll stay open a bit longer."

"All right then. Be as quick as you can."

She slipped out of the car and crept towards the gates. Fortunately, the house was a long way down the drive, which was lined with fat lime trees planted on two grassy banks. These would make great cover, thought Rachel.

There was also a majestic stone keep between the gates and the mansion, closer to the building. It looked like the front of a mini castle. There were two spiky octagonal turrets. One on the left and one on the right, with slit windows and an arched entrance in the middle which had a metal gate fixed into the centre. The great thing from her perspective was that it concealed her from the gaze of the house.

As Rachel looked down the long path of the estate, she heard the electronic gates clang shut behind her. The sound made her jump.

A split second later, she realised she was alone on the inside. Lake's face appeared at the gate. His hands tried to prise the huge metal bars apart. But it was too late. The estate was well and truly locked down.

CHAPTER 19

Rachel listened hard. She thought she could hear wheels churning on the ground. Then she saw two young boys riding up the drive on bicycles. The taller one rode more confidently but with a wobble here and there. They both wore long orange trousers, green T-shirts and sandals.

The boys wove around the stone structure at the centre of the drive, crunching the gravel with their wheels. One went to the left and one to the right. They approached Rachel at a leisurely pace, concentrating hard. They had a huge distance to cover, giving Rachel time to update Lake.

"I can see two small boys. They're over there, down the drive. Can you see?"

"Oh, yeah. I see them."

"I think I'm going to be all right. I can handle a couple of school kids."

"There is no way I am leaving you in there – are you a complete lunatic? We need to be careful. They might be all right, but this guy, Daniel, is probably their dad. We don't know what he's capable of. Or rather, we do, if the Metropolitan's anything to go by. Wait for me while I find a way over the fence."

"Fine then. You look for a way in. But if I can find a way of getting them to open the gates, listen out, and we can go in together."

"Deal."

"But, you know what? I have a feeling I'll be all right." Rachel smiled as the small boys came near. Two pairs of eyes stared at Rachel under two mops of messy brown hair.

The older one called out, "Who goes there? Friend or foe?" He had a big, confident voice.

Rachel smiled. "Friend."

"Surrender or die," he added.

"Surrender."

"And what about the man?"

"What man?" asked Rachel, gently.

"We saw you. On the TV." The younger one had a quieter voice but was also confident and stared hard at her.

"I'm sorry?"

"Rory means we saw you on our 'close-circle' television security system from the house. We have CCTV cameras everywhere because Dad knows everything about technology. And security."

"Oh, I see. Yes, the man's my friend. I wonder if you could just open these gates so I can nip back out to him? I kind of got trapped. They closed on me."

"We're not allowed to play with the gates," said the younger boy named Rory. "Are we Cam?"

"Don't tell my name. Now she knows my name. Mum says we shouldn't tell strangers our names," complained the older boy.

"But you already told her mine. I heard you. You said, 'Rory means...'!"

"It's okay, boys. Don't fight about it. I'm not going to tell anyone your names. I promise. So, how old are you both?"

"I am Cameron, and I'm seven and a half. Rory is six."

"Well, I guess I'm pleased to meet you. I'm Rachel."

The boys stared at her and started pulling funny faces. She wondered what on earth had got into them.

Suddenly, a third voice spoke. Rachel realised there was someone else standing next to her. A young man had crept up and was just behind her and to one side. He gently took her arm, making her jump.

She turned her torso to look at him and saw the most beautiful face she had ever seen outside a Hollywood movie. He was about a foot taller than Rachel and had dreamy almond-shaped eyes and long lashes, a strong, wide jaw, and dark, wavy hair. She wondered whether he could tell she was swooning on the inside.

"Rachel Race," he said in a deep and musical voice. "We mean you no harm. However, I do need you to come with me to the house."

Rachel sighed audibly. "Okay…" Anticipation and fear gripped her heart.

"Micah," said the young man, who could have been eighteen or nineteen years of age, around the same age as Lake. "I am the personal assistant to Daniel William Harcourt. This is his family home, as I am sure you are aware since you are either visiting or trespassing."

"Oh," said Rachel dumbly. "Visiting, really."

Micah relaxed a little. "I believe you have met Mister Harcourt once before. But regardless of that, you will find him a changed man."

"Really? How lovely." Rachel realised she was using her breathy, girly voice.

"First, why not give Lake Emerson a shout and tell him you have been invited to dinner and that he should go home."

"Oh, I don't think he'll go for that. He can be quite persistent."

"Why not give it a try? Besides, it would be nice to compare notes on the Initiation, and I'm sure Lake isn't really interested in all that, is he?"

"No, you're probably right. Give me a moment, would you?" She smiled at the young boys and leant back towards the gate to call out to Lake.

Although she wasn't fully convinced of her own safety, Rachel insisted to Lake that she wanted him to leave her alone, arguing that she believed nothing bad would happen to her. After all, she'd sat face to face with Samyaza, not that she told Lake that.

If anything happened, he knew where she was, and she had her mobile with her. Rachel stood her ground, and eventually, Lake relented. As she walked away, she felt like she had paid him back a little for the stuff with that Kumi girl. Rachel smiled.

☙ 12345 ❧

CALEB STEPPED out into the pleasant tropical heat of Santa Cruz de la Sierra, Bolivia. Viru Viru International Airport was behind him: a long, flat building with dark windows divided into rectangular sections. Across the front of the airport were the words 'Aeropuerto Internacional Viru-Viru' in big blue italic letters on white panels. An aeroplane soared overhead, leaving behind a throaty roar.

Caleb had never visited Bolivia before. He had travelled to Brazil several times and Chile once, which bordered Bolivia. But he had never seen Bolivia, which touched on Peru, Paraguay, Argentina, and Chile.

Santa Cruz is Bolivia's largest city, with La Paz being the second. The city of Santa Cruz dates back to 1560. It was, for a hundred and fifty years or so, located over two hundred kilometres east of its current location. But in the seventeenth century, the city was moved to its present position, just east of the Cordillera Oriental foothills. When Caleb learned of this on the long plane journey, he imagined the citizens banding together, each taking a piece of the city and dragging it into place, much like you would with a trampoline or a tent.

From the air, Santa Cruz was a set of concentric circles resembling the cross-section of a tree trunk. These roads radiated from Principal Plaza at the heart of the city, with arterial routes directing traffic from one area to another, all within a grid-like street system.

Caleb's airport taxi followed one of these arterial roads into the centre of town to pick up his hire car, an ancient, oversized American wreck. It had a broad bonnet and an endless trunk, and it rocked as it rolled. For Caleb, it was perfect for his purposes—a big vehicle for a big country, capable of transporting him southeast, out of town, to where the hotel on the matchbook was located.

He felt drugged by the tropical atmosphere: warm air drenched with wet heat, which made his very bones sluggish. As he drove, he noticed the city had a few tall buildings and was very green.

He spotted a few sloths in the trees, which were strange furry creatures with long limbs.

Beyond the outskirts of the city, he could glimpse the vast Amazonian plains stretching as far as the eye could see: a carpet of broccoli-like trees. He thought about eating at a place that served Brazilian-style meat on a spit but opted for local Bolivian cuisine instead. A friendly-looking diner at the side of the road welcomed him in. It had half a dozen tables and handwritten menus and smelled of chillies and hot rice.

He sat down and ordered *Picante de Pollo*. It was chicken in a red-hot salsa served with a portion of rice and cassava. Shortly after, the café owner placed the plate in front of him with a warm "*Buen provecho*" ("enjoy your meal") and brought him a refreshing *somó*, a cold white corn drink. It was the right balance for the salsa, which was proving to be challenging for Caleb's mouth.

He paid and went back to his rental, which was parked on the road outside. There were three men in his car, sitting and waiting. One was lounging in the passenger seat, and two slouched in the back, and it looked as though they had broken in without smashing any windows.

"Interesting," murmured Caleb.

He paused at the diner door, put on his round sunglasses, and said under his breath, "Dunamis, my friend, I'm going to need your help on this one."

⤙ *12345* ⤚

It was a surreal experience walking along the drive and past the stone mini-castle construction. Rachel had gone from trespasser to guest in an instant. Here she was, heading towards her enemy, with a gracious and angelically handsome man by her side and accompanied by two cherubs on bikes. It was very surreal.

The walk to the mansion was made even more pleasant by the warm summer evening. Two bright butterflies came close to her cheek, and she chose not to flinch.

As Rachel walked down the gravel driveway, past the lime trees, she came to a long swathe of cut grass. It stretched out before the house like a carpet. She observed two white goblet-shaped flowerpots on the corners of the grass near the residence.

Windows stretched out on either side of a doorway that jutted outwards, making it distinct from the line of the house. The mansion itself was on three levels with gabled bedrooms at the top.

They came to the arched doorway, with a massive black door recessed into it.

Daniel was waiting for them in a jacket and tie with an elegant lady by his side. She had on a lovely blue evening dress with flowing lines that caught the evening sun.

"Welcome to our home, Rachel. This is my wife, Arabella. I see you've already met Micah and my children, Cameron and Rory."

"You are very welcome, Rachel," said Arabella in a kind voice. "You must have so many questions, but I want you to know that we are friends, and you are, of course, free to leave at any time. I hope that you will come inside and talk for a while, though."

There was something of a stand-off for several long seconds. Arabella smiled at Rachel, staring at her with her intense blue eyes. Daniel looked at his children as though embarrassed. The children fidgeted.

Rachel's emotions swirled around, with invisible butterflies rising from her stomach to her throat and back down again. Anxiety tugged at her organs. If she stayed, she would be dragged further into the unknown.

But her curiosity won the day. "That would be nice."

"Would you like to stay for dinner? It will be ready soon," asked Arabella. "It would be our pleasure."

Rachel nodded and mumbled, "Love to." She immediately felt underdressed.

"Wonderful. The boys can give you the grand tour of the inside of the house if you like?"

Daniel added, "Lytescote is an exquisite house, which has been in my wife's family for many years. Generations, in fact. It has a sixteenth-century timber frame, a slate roof, and lime plaster. But listen to me going on. Please come in."

Rachel hesitated for a moment. Seeing this, Daniel said, "It looks like your friend has gone home now, so there's no need to worry about that. You are perfectly safe here."

Rachel had a brief anxious thought about whether Lake had actually gone home or was still lurking about. Then she followed Daniel and Arabella into the house, followed by Micah and the children.

❧ 12345 ❧

THE MEN SEEMED to be in no hurry. Caleb watched as a policeman went up to the car. He looked at the men and glanced over at Caleb, who was across the road outside the diner. The policeman was dressed in a green military-style shirt and trousers, black boots and sunglasses.

He spoke to the men in Bolivian Spanish, which was slightly

alien to Caleb's ears. He was familiar with Spanish but knew that this was a variation of the language in the Lowlands.

The man in the front seat greeted the officer with a firm "*buenas tardes*" ("good day"), extending his hand for a strong handshake while maintaining steady eye contact throughout.

They exchanged a few words, and the man handed the official a packet of cigarettes. Shortly, the policeman walked away, whistling. The man in the back seat had forced down his window and spat at the pavement outside.

"Okay," said Caleb to himself. He took a deep breath, sauntered over to his car, opened the door, and took his seat at the wheel. Continuing to ignore the men, he put his key into the ignition.

He started the engine and pulled away. Once he was moving, he kept his eyes fixed on the road ahead, following it southeast out of the city.

As the breeze came in through the open windows, he said quietly, "Servants of Samyaza. You are here to direct me to my friends. I am going the right way, yes?"

"Shut up and drive," growled the man next to him. He produced a slice of dried beef jerky and started to chew on it. Meanwhile, the beautiful Bolivian scenery flowed by, and Santa Cruz gradually shrank from a bustling city to a small town, then to a village, and finally to a distant dot on the horizon.

⌇ 12345 ⌇

RACHEL IMMEDIATELY FELL in love with Lytescote Manor. It was so beautiful and old inside, with so many features that linked it to centuries past. She saw a grandfather clock, ancient fireplaces, and beautiful pottery. Imposing dark chunks of wooden furniture were contrasted with gold and silver treasures that shone out from the mantelpieces.

Daniel, Arabella, and Micah quickly disappeared to attend to their own matters. Cameron and Rory remained to show her around and amuse her with interesting stories about the house. They had moved in last year but had clearly visited frequently through their short lives, so they knew it well.

They knew every hiding place and each tiny mark of surreptitious graffiti left by generations of mischievous children. They made her crawl under a table to see one mark, which they said went back over three hundred years.

They informed Rachel that one set of lively children used to play a game where they weighed themselves on giant scales before and after dinner. The one who put on the most weight won the game. One of their ancestors, a boy, had put on half a stone in one sitting, making him the winner of the game. Rory laughed out loud and then covered his mouth with his hands, his eyes glistening.

Although Rachel didn't visit every one of them, she learned that there were fifteen bedrooms, some upstairs and some down in the basement. She came across long halls and a grand library with books up to the ceiling. She passed through the billiard room, which was now the toy room. She saw chandeliers, ornate gilded mirrors, and paintings from Elizabethan through to Victorian, as well as exquisite drapes, pelmet boards, and over-mantels.

Rachel passed through countless incredible rooms on her grand tour, seeing stately red and gold chairs everywhere. Before long, she had built up an appetite for dinner. Still, they walked.

There were dining and drawing rooms, utility rooms, and function rooms. There was even a Victorian chamber for growing oranges, which they called an orangery.

"So, would a room for growing lemons be called a lemony?" she asked.

"Don't be silly," said Cameron, laughing at her humour.

However, Cameron informed her that his distant relatives had built the house after dismantling a medieval manor hall nearby. He even showed her their initials on the stone chimney-piece in the dining room. Next to these was a date: 1576.

Partway down a long staircase, Rachel plucked up the courage to ask Rory a more personal question. Cameron had already descended to the bottom.

"Your father, what's he like?"

"He's the best dad in the world."

"Mm," nodded Rachel. They reached the bottom of the staircase. Rachel caught her breath as she saw Micah standing there. He had changed into a formal shirt with a collar and a sports jacket and was ready for the evening meal. Rachel smiled when she saw him, her heart jumping like a salmon leaping upstream. Again, she felt extremely underdressed to sit down and eat with these people.

"Dinner is ready. But first, your friend is still at the gates and is being rather persistent. Perhaps you could have a word with him, and then we can eat?

Rachel blushed. "Sorry."

"Please follow me."

❧ 12345 ❧

THE MEN in the car were not good conversationalists. In fact, they spoke very little, which suited Caleb as he was used to long periods of silence himself. The man next to him grunted phrases like "left at the next turning" and "take a right over there." Apart from that, Caleb had been able to enjoy the stunning scenery in peace.

The men had not threatened him in any way. Not yet. In essence, they were hitching a ride and directing his journey. They didn't appear to be armed, and nobody brandished a pistol. He could eject them onto the tarmac and drive on, but equally, he didn't want to take any chances. They knew where to go, which was a provision of sorts.

As they drove further away from Santa Cruz, the surrounding countryside became more rural. There were more fields and farms and fewer buildings. Light green and brown tufty fronds of grass grew near the road. Thick green trees stretched into the distance. Almost immediately upon leaving the city, the poverty of the place became apparent. Many people lived in simple-looking white or dust-red bungalows with flat roofs. Some buildings were mud brown with thatched roofs. There was an absence of conspicuous wealth: big cars, satellite dishes, swimming pools, and the like.

Caleb watched a father and son team drive their dappled cow and cart along the side of the road. The cart, a slab of wood, had huge metal wheels, hand-beaten and uneven. It bore green leafy crops. The man had a small, black, rounded hat with a brown scarf tied around the base. The young boy held a long stick and walked barefoot. Through the open windows flowed the smell of warm air over harvested crops.

Caleb looked at his travelling companions in his rear-view mirror. They were natives, brown and weathered, and used to the outdoors. There was nothing particularly menacing about them except for their dark glasses. They were more likely to be farmers than gangsters. The man beside him wore a baseball cap and big sunglasses and chewed at his dried beef from time to time.

For all their posturing, they may well be nice guys looking forward to receiving some cash in their calloused hands. Apart from the fact that they had broken into his car and were giving him directions, they may as well have been hitchhikers. Caleb had seen far worse.

What concerned him more was that the Dunamis had grown increasingly silent. This happened to Caleb periodically as he walked with the Dunamis, especially when he ignored its advice and went his own way—something he tried to avoid these days. But this time, he had received the warning in New York. "There are times when silence has the loudest voice. You will not hear me for a time, but when that time comes, do not doubt that I am with you."

Maybe this was as the angel had indicated: the time for silence. If so, it would be a deafening silence. At the end of the day, Caleb was just a man and not a superhero. Without the power of the Dunamis, he would quickly come to the end of his own resources.

It was time to dig deep and have faith that everything would turn out okay.

CHAPTER 20

Rachel had a tense and vocal argument with Lake at the gates of Lytescote Manor, which sent him storming off home with the words, "Suit yourself: it's your funeral." After taking a few minutes to compose herself, Rachel returned to the house and was met by Micah at the front door.

"Miss Race, dinner is served," he said with a smile.

At the table, nobody quizzed her about the incident with Lake, so she swiftly put it to the back of her mind. She enjoyed the meal much more than the one she had endured with Samyaza the other day. The children kept her amused with their wriggling and giggling and funny observations. She stole glimpses of Micah as often as she could when he wasn't looking. Although he wasn't particularly warm towards her, it was enough to be sitting at a table with such a great-looking guy. When he paid her any attention, she glowed like an energy bulb.

Daniel and Arabella were excellent hosts, attentive and charming. They made her feel comfortable, particularly Arabella, who sensed her awkwardness and instinctively drew the conversation away from her at those points.

They ate a Scottish smoked salmon starter, with a main course of Griffton saddle of lamb and fresh local vegetables.

Arabella had prepared the food, and Daniel had chosen the drinks. It was the sort of cuisine you would pay big money for at a top-quality restaurant, the sort of restaurant her dad never had the money to take her to.

There was a lot of small talk and very little reference to the events of last year. It was almost as though they had adopted her into the family and always dined together. The boys talked about their school and what they were learning. She found out some interesting facts about the human body, aquatic mammals, and interplanetary space travel. She found out that Cameron would like to live on Jupiter, but Rory would be happy to have a house on Pluto. As for her, she answered she was just fine living on the Earth.

When the spotlight turned to her, she spoke politely of her work at Nightshift and Rock and Shock. Arabella said a little about her family history in relation to the house. Daniel himself remained quiet but smiled graciously whenever he passed Rachel a dish or offered to top up her elderflower cordial.

The third course, dessert, was her favourite course of all. She got to choose from three different ones and opted to have two of them. Nobody objected. One was a mini tartlet with glazed fruit, and the other was a strawberry, blueberry, and kiwi slice. The other was a lemon and lime sorbet. She hadn't eaten this well for weeks.

The meal ended, and they moved to an adjoining lounge that smelt of rose petals. It was decorated with red and gold silk and wide, cushioned seats and couches.

They carried their drinks with them and placed them on their respective tables. Each had a candle on it so that the room glowed with discreet lighting. Rachel chose a comfortable seat in the corner and put her elderflower cordial down next to her. The couple took their places on a sofa, with Micah selecting a matching chair. He extended his long legs out in front of him, closed his eyes, relaxed, and smiled. Rachel tried not to stare.

"We have been waiting for you for some time," said Daniel

after a long sip of his wine. Rachel felt self-conscious and held her glass in both hands, smiling nervously.

"I didn't know when you would come, but I was certain you would. Saying that, I am curious, how did you come to find our house?"

Rachel babbled, "That's a good question and one which I'd love to be able to explain. It was Lake, actually. My, er, friend. Someone gave him your details and your work address. We kind of followed you here in secret."

"You stalked me?" asked Daniel, but Rachel saw he was grinning. "In secret, in a noisy old white Nissan Micra, following two vehicles back all the way from Griffton town centre?"

"Yeah, that was us. How did you guess?" Daniel and Arabella smiled at the same time.

"Daniel knows a little bit about surveillance," Arabella said. "Somebody gave your friend my details. Do you mind if I ask who that was? "

"A girl. She calls herself Kumiko. She's about my age, maybe a bit older. I don't really know. I do know she's a liar, though."

"I am not familiar with her. Not from my past life. She sounds like a new recruit for Samyaza."

"So, you do know Samyaza?" asked Rachel quickly.

"I knew Samyaza. Past tense. I served him. That was when you met me. I was serving him against my will. All followers of Samyaza end up doing that in the end, if they didn't from the beginning."

Daniel continued, "You found me at a time when I thought I had got rid of him. But he was waiting, biding his time for years. It's true. I allowed myself to be used by him like so many times before." Daniel frowned.

"With this in mind, I need to ask you something, Rachel. I am really very sorry for what happened to you last year. Will you forgive me for my part in everything that happened? I know it's a big request, but I need to ask it. Forgive me for giving you that bag with the powder for the bomb that led to the tragedy, my connection with the men in the house, and my part in your imprisonment? Please forgive me. I beg you. It must have been horrible for you."

"Yeah, it was. But, sure, why not? You seem like nice folk, and it's all in the past now, isn't it?"

⌒ 12345 ⌒

A LITTLE LATER, Daniel was saying, "By now, you will know what he's like and what he's capable of. He came back into my life after years. He sucked me right back in. The problem is that once you've given your life to him, he owns you: body and soul. He's worse than a drug addiction or any addiction you can think of. Those things are far easier to break free from."

Rachel sat there with her big eyes open, unblinking.

"So, I formulated a plan of my own. I determined to take my own life and be rid of him for good. It seemed the only way to be free. But I learnt that there is another way."

Rachel nodded for him to continue.

"Samyaza wanted to destroy me. He wants to destroy all of us. But the Rescuer had another way, a way that gave me life and freedom, though I really didn't deserve it."

"You met the Dunamis?" whispered Rachel, though it was more of a statement, a realisation.

"Yes," said Daniel quietly. "And he introduced me to the Rescuer." Rachel gasped audibly. The four of them sat in the warm orange glow of the candles, lost in the labyrinth of their own thoughts.

But Daniel hadn't finished. "That was when I met Caleb Noble, who became my friend from then on. He was there when I died. And he was there when I came back to life, to a new life. And you know him, don't you?"

"Yes, I met him last year. He got me out of that cell."

"Then, I imagine you also met the Dunamis?"

Rachel sat in silence. Everything she'd experienced last year was real. There was no more pretending.

"Yes. I met him in the old house near the cliff."

"So then, you will know deep down inside you, in your heart of hearts, that what I'm saying is true. The thing is, Rachel, you were made for a purpose. Life isn't completely random, with no sense or meaning. You were made for adventure and a life lived to the full. The Rescuer loves you and values you, and I want you to know that there is hope for you. Your life has a meaning. There's a reason you were born as the person you were born, in this part of the world, in Griffton. There is hope for you and a future."

Rachel remembered Samyaza's words, a pale reflection of Daniel's. Samyaza had said, "There is a plan for you and a future. And it's with us," but his words had filled her with dread.

As Daniel spoke his words, they had an authority that resonated. She relaxed into her chair and listened more. His words were soothing balm for her heart.

Daniel went on, "I did some terrible things for Samyaza, some of them because he forced me to, but a lot of the time, my own darkness compelled me. I deserved to be punished for all the things I did to people. I was an enemy of the good King and a servant of Samyaza. My training taught me to hate anything that was good. Hate it with a passion."

"But just when I thought that all was lost, the Rescuer embraced me and turned me around. He gave me a fresh start and invited me to be part of his adventure. Caleb taught me about friendship with the Dunamis, how to hear him, and how to walk in step with him. And do you know what? I no longer fear anyone." Daniel laughed out loud. "Because wherever the Dunamis is, there is freedom: real freedom."

"Don't fear anyone, Rachel. What can people do? Cause you pain, even destroy your body? Believe me, I know. No, you need to fear the one who can destroy your soul. Choose your sides carefully. And be on guard against Samyaza and his unholy hordes."

"But who is the Dunamis, and where does he come from?" Rachel blurted out.

"He has always existed. But he was sent from the one who lived and died and lives. The one who paid the highest price. The Rescuer."

"I know him. I dream about him. He's a warrior on a gigantic horse with a long sword, and he travels with a group of fighting men. The sky is purple, and there are mountains all around."

"That's him. And at the appointed time, he's coming back." Rachel nodded, utterly confused.

"Well, it sounds like we're all on the same page now," said Micah.

"Maybe we are, and maybe we're not. I still have lots of questions," Rachel complained.

"I'm afraid they are going to have to wait," Daniel interjected. "First, we need to compare notes about the Initiation."

"It's late now, but if you like, you can stay over in one of our spare rooms. Or we could drop you back home if you have to get up early for work?" Arabella interjected.

Rachel turned to Arabella and smiled in surprise. "That would be lovely if it's no bother." The thought of being away from home and her dad, even for one night, filled her with relief. Coupled with this was the enjoyment she felt just being in the company of these strange people. It was reminiscent of being in the presence of the Dunamis last year.

"So, the Initiation," said Daniel, bringing them back on track. Rachel told them, "All I know is that there was a story. It was about a doorway between this world and another. It's a portal in the mountains. I had some dreams, maybe visions about some mountains. The Himalayas in Nepal. They were in pain. They split open, and something deep inside the Earth was roaring. I don't really like to think about it, to be honest, but there it is."

"Ah, I see that you're prophetic. You have dreams." Daniel exchanged looks with Micah. "Go on, please."

"I also know the story goes that Samyaza is planning to climb back out somehow and take over the world with his bad guys, the unholy hordes as you call them."

"The Watchers: the Grigori, and their Nephilim. Caleb was right," said Daniel to Micah.

"The Initiation took place a year ago, not that time is significant in this case. What we need to ascertain is how the stone head is linked to the Initiation," said Micah.

"Samyaza also took my finger. You knew about that, didn't you?" Rachel shot at Daniel.

"Actually, I didn't. Unfortunately, I don't know what the significance of your finger is. Apart from, perhaps, that Samyaza was trying to blackmail you to do his will. He usually tries to go after family members, but maybe that time..." Daniel stopped as he realised Rachel was looking deeply unhappy.

"I thought maybe I was someone special," Rachel whispered. She hadn't really meant to say it out loud, but it was now out in the open. "I thought he chose me because I was important to everything that was happening."

"Oh, but you are, Rachel," Arabella insisted. "Everybody is special and significant. What Daniel said is true. We each have a different role to play."

"So, I lost my finger for no reason?" Rachel started to feel wet streaks down her cheeks, and her face was hot.

"No, I didn't say that. Knowing Samyaza, he had a reason far more profound than that he just wanted to get you on board. All I'm saying is that for now, we don't know what his reason is."

"One thing we do know is that Caleb is travelling to New York to find out what needs to be done next. Beyond that, we know very little," said Micah. Rachel was again struck by his beauty, the line of his jaw in the candlelight, and the way his almond-shaped eyes sparkled. She knew she was being unfair to Lake, but he had his horrible little Kumi to swoon over.

"I think we've gone as far as we can tonight, and we all need some rest," said Daniel. "Only one thing remains. Can we agree, Rachel, to work together?"

They all turned to stare at Rachel, who was wiping her eyes. "Me? You're asking me to join whatever this is?"

"Yes," said Micah. "It's essential that you're either all in or all out. There is no in-between. We don't want to give Samyaza an inch. So, are you in?"

"Yes. Count me in." Rachel gave him her best smile.

CALEB DROVE the men deep into the countryside. Soybean and coca crops lined the roads for miles. Solitary birds specked the clear blue sky. An unaccompanied coal-black dog ran alongside the car at one point, gave up the chase, and sat down. Every so often, farmers paused from their labour to stand and stare.

The road wound through a village and along to its outskirts, passing yet more fields. Eventually, the men directed Caleb to turn onto a smaller path that led uphill. A scraggy field lined a mud path that led them past several storehouses and up to a wide farm building.

Caleb immediately recognised the men outside the farm as being 'Sapana' Dream Fighters. The servants of Samyaza had dark leather tunics decorated with a diagonal sash and their hall-mark swords. He had encountered them in Nepal, Slovakia, and half a dozen other places.

"I see. So, they've made their way here now."

Then Caleb glimpsed a couple of young lads dressed up as Dream Fighters. They hung back shyly and stared with big round eyes in hairless faces. By their posture, Caleb knew they were trying to be mean and strong. He knew instinctively they had been beguiled by the warriors, who no doubt had come as knights in shining armour.

Caleb's companions left him in the car, and one of the Dream Fighters handed their leader a fistful of notes. Content with this, the men nodded at the Dream Fighters and sloped off down the hill. Nobody stopped them. Caleb assumed this had been the arrangement from the start.

He sat in the heat of the hire car and waited, feeling like a parcel that had been dumped outside someone's door. A fly buzzed around his head, and he watched it escape the car and ascend.

After a long time, his old friends were brought out through the front door. He could have attempted to escape down the hill but would no doubt have been quickly restrained.

They were alive.

Caleb cried out, "Hey! Anton! Eli! You're here! Are you okay?"

Eli replied, "Yeah, we're okay! I see you got the taxi service as well!"

"Taxi? That's my hire car. Well, it was my hire car. Not sure if I'll ever get to return it to Santa Cruz."

Anton was around the same age as Caleb, in his mid-forties, though he looked older. He had fluffy, flyaway hair, metal spectacles, and a lanky and self-conscious stature compared with Caleb's muscular frame. He had given Caleb a huge, goofy smile when he saw him and shrugged his thin shoulders.

Although the men looked as though they had been beaten, Eli called out cheerfully, "Wonderful to see you, young Caleb. I can't really complain. After all, I have had plenty of time to catch up with Anton!"

Eli's long white hair was matted, and his beard was unkempt. But for a man in his seventies, he looked remarkably well, perhaps even better than many men in their middle years.

Anton said, "You're looking well, Caleb. Glad you decided to drop in. I don't suppose you brought any of my whisky with you? I'm sure we could all do with a 'wee dram.'"

Eli smiled and laughed with his eyes. A Dream Fighter shoved him roughly from behind his shoulder blade, and he winced.

"Hey! That's no way to treat an old man," shouted Caleb.

"You are enemies of Samyaza, and we will treat you as we wish," he snapped.

"The only power you have is the power the Rescuer allows you," replied Anton. This won him a punch in the mouth from one of the warriors, which drew blood.

"Dunamis?" asked Caleb quietly.

Eli and Anton shook their heads. "All quiet," said Eli.

Anton caught Caleb up in a hushed and hurried whisper. The Dream Fighters had arrived at his house in Jura and kept him waiting with a bag over his head while they helped themselves to his possessions. Then, they led him on a long walk over the hills near the village. He remembered little other than walking a great distance without food or water and finally being allowed to see daylight again. He could see from the window that he was in a strange land, Bolivia, but he had to work this out for himself.

As for Eli, he had arrived at Santa Cruz but had walked right into the custody of the Dream Fighters' henchmen, such was the corruption at the airport. They drove him out to the farmhouse, and he had been under guard with Anton ever since.

The front door of the farmhouse swung open, and a huge Dream Fighter in leather armour and a red and black sash came striding out. He was an imposing figure with a fierce countenance, but the three men were not afraid of him, having faced men like him before. They were well aware of their own limitations and how much they relied on the Dunamis for protection.

The warrior stood still and stared at them in disgust. He had a robust face and looked like he had shaved with a broken bottle. His neck and cheeks were raw and rutted.

He said through gritted teeth, "A message from Samyaza. Your comrades in Griffton who oppose my plans are being taken care of. As a gift to me, they are all in one place. This makes them so much easier for me to crush."

Then, turning to one of his warriors, the lead Dream Fighter ordered: "Take them."

He barked at the men to walk, and the two Dream Fighter guards placed their hands on their sword hilts to show they meant business. Caleb quickly made a calculation and decided against trying to take them on.

Then, seeing José and Diego hanging around by the wall of the house, the chief said, "You two. Lead the way to the stone head." The two boys snapped to attention, revitalised with their orders. They pushed past the three men and started to walk slowly away from their house.

As they walked ahead, Caleb noticed that one of the boys had a missing finger. It was the fourth finger of his left hand.

⚬~ 12345 ~⚬

RACHEL STAYED the night at Lytescote Manor as they had requested. Her room was beautiful and interesting, and she had an adjoining bathroom. There were many things to pick up and look at, ornaments and relics from distant lands and times.

The family slept in the west wing of the house, which had a series of rooms connected by a long corridor. The boys had chosen to share a room even though there were many available for them. They just liked each other's company. Micah also lived with the family. Rachel learned he was an orphan with some sort of feudal attachment to Arabella's family that spanned generations.

She was enjoying the long moments she was getting to share with him. He had a sharp mind, was quick to make logical connections, and unravelled passing intrigues. He seemed to have an innate understanding of Rachel and what she was about, as though he had been studying her for some time. For example, he said rather knowingly at one point, "Of course, you would say that, considering what you've been through." Rachel wondered if he was toying with her.

He also maintained a sort of professional distance, recognising his role in the family as a personal assistant to the head of the household.

"I very much enjoy my work here with Mr Harcourt. Considering all the responsibilities he bears, with his work and home life, I have great admiration and respect for him."

Towards the end of the evening, they found themselves alone, sitting in the candlelight and talking about life. She watched the flickering flame trace his jawline and make his beautiful eyes sparkle. Then, with no warning, he seemed to grow bored with the conversation and drew things to a conclusion. It was as if he wanted to be rid of her.

And so, with a brief and formal, "Good night to you, Miss Race," he disappeared to his quarters. Rachel sat there speechless, feeling utterly rejected.

In the night, she dreamt of the Rescuer on a moonlight-white horse. He was in the midst of a ferocious battle beneath an apocalyptic sky. He was slaying horrible nightmare creatures, disfigured by aggression and pride. Nothing could stop them but the double edge of his blade and the swords of his fighters.

The Rescuer gripped the reins with his left hand as blood dripped from his sword and up his right arm. Meanwhile, his host of angelic warriors were also engaged in combat. Bloodcurdling screams rose on all sides as their enemy pressed them hard at the top of a ridge that led down into a verdant, misty valley.

The Rescuer skilfully drew back his arm, his strong biceps flexing as he swung back the sword, rotating his shoulder and torso as he did so. He reached the end of the movement and brought the sword forward with all his might. It cut a swathe through the air and connected with his enemy, a snarling beast with murder in its hard black eyes. It flashed its teeth, showing spittle-covered fangs, and brought a massive, clawed hand up to swipe back.

With a mighty roar and an outstretched arm, the mighty king finished his foe, completing another rescue mission. His men caught their breath and regrouped. They looked around them at the scattered remains of leathery, winged monsters that had met their end. There were bodies everywhere. It wasn't a war they had chosen, but they were determined to end it.

The fighting was done, and the enemy was destroyed. The Rescuer and his army rode slowly into the valley in search of water for their steeds. Tomorrow's battle lay ahead of them through the green valley and onwards into the swirling violet mists.

⤜ 12345 ⤛

BENSON WAS COWERING in his bed in the middle of the night. He was like a little boy afraid of the dark, peeking over the edge of his duvet at the moonlit shadows.

"You and I have been on a journey," Samyaza was saying to him. "We had some fun, we've played some tricks, we've done some damage."

Benson jabbered like a baboon. "No… I… But…"

"To be honest with you, Benson, I don't like you, and I never have. You let me down. You're weak, and you're a mess. The long and short of it is I can't work with you anymore. I just have that final job for you to do before we go our separate ways. You're going to make a call and say the words I give you to say. Okay?"

"Okay. Okay, okay. And then you leave?"

"That's the deal." The hideous demon was a dark, contorted smudge in his mind's eye. But he was more real than anything Benson had ever known. He desperately wished he had never met Samyaza, this repugnant nightmare creature who utterly controlled him. The idea of true liberation was so appealing. It compelled him to make this final call.

"Stevie? It's Steel. Everyone awake? Good. It's time to go. Remember your orders. Be quick, be alert and be careful. Leave no survivors. You won't hear from me again. Call my associate when it's done. I assume she told you everything you need to know? Good. I've made arrangements for her to settle with you afterwards. That's all."

CHAPTER 21

Stevie Teeth assembled his motley crew of Zodiacs in the chilly night air. They were standing outside the eastern fence of the estate. Pig was by his side, looking eerily psychotic in the moonlight. In front of them fidgeted two dozen, eager young thugs. They chattered to each other, sneering, taunting, and joking with excitement, rubbing their hands to get warm.

"Zodiacs," began Stevie. "I've brought you all together tonight to do a job. It's what we do best. We do some damage and slap some people about. In other words, have some fun. It's easy for us, and we love it. We were born for it."

The crowd laughed and sneered.

"This time, there's money in it for you. Decent cash. Money that folds that will keep you in beer for a week. I'll give it to you at the end if you're still alive, that is." They laughed again.

"So, marching orders. We grab our tools, scale the fence, have a look around, and then go into the house. Our aim isn't to smash it up, though you can if you want. What we need to do is find the people in there and end them. Every last one. We do what we have to, and then we get out. Everyone clear?"

There was some murmuring and lots of nodding, with nobody objecting.

"Right then. Robbie and Smiler, pop your balaclavas on. You're going up this fence to have a look. Spread out a bit and grab a mate to get you up. Come back and tell me what you see. We'll take it from there. Go."

Stevie added, "You two, Tes and Doggo, you're next. Grab some guys and go and have a look down the end and see if we're better off going for the back of the house. Got it? Good. Now go."

A GRANDFATHER CLOCK TICKED. Computer fans whirred quietly. The children breathed deeply in their sleep. Rachel was dreaming noiselessly about the mountains. But Daniel was awake. He was watching the twenty-four-hour news in his study when he glimpsed, on his computer screen, some activity outside the gates of the mansion.

Immediately, he flipped more security screens on and panned the outdoor cameras to get a better picture. Men in black clothing and balaclavas were climbing the outer fence of the estate. He didn't wait to see what sort of weapons they had. Instead, he tapped on his keyboard to initiate the security measures he had put into place. If working for Samyaza had taught him one thing, it was to expect the unexpected and be prepared. Coupled with this, he had been prompted by the Dunamis last autumn to erect the security fence around the property, and now he understood why. He just hoped he'd thought of everything.

Daniel made a habit of knowing exactly where his important things were. These included his wallet, keys, bank cards, cash, passports, and digital storage containing copies of everything from business documents to family photos. Soon, these were in his big leather backpack, along with a multipurpose knife and a light.

He trotted up to the bedroom, woke Arabella gently, and went to his walk-in wardrobe to change out of his pyjamas. Next, he woke everyone else up quickly.

Very quickly.

⚯ 12345 ⚯

THE OUTER FENCE was a towering metal barrier that encircled the house and its inner gardens. But the Zodiacs were pleased to discover they could throw their ropes up and over, securing them for the climb. Robbie, who was chosen for reconnaissance, clambered up onto his big friend Toby's shoulders to look over the fence. He complained that they should have brought ladders with them, but once up, he had a good view into the garden.

He waved to Smiler, who was further along the fence, on another Zodiac's shoulders. Smiler gave Robbie a thumbs-up sign. Robbie shivered in the midnight air. Out here in the countryside, there were no streetlights, but the property was well-lit by the moon. Through the slit in his balaclava, he looked across the massive distance between the outer fence and the mansion. Memories of being a lookout in his Glasgow housing estate came back to him.

He could see well-kept gardens in the distance, over the fields, and something that looked like a mini-castle building near the house. This was a square construction with turrets at the top. The house itself was a large three-floor building with lots of windows and chimneys. There were tall trees all around, which could give them places to hide if they needed it.

Between where he stood and the house, across the fields between, was a second barrier, a low wall. That one would be much easier to get over. After that, he felt that breaking into the house should be simple enough.

Robbie glanced down and thought it looked a long way to

jump, though the bushes on the other side might be helpful. He could break his legs if he fell badly. He decided to keep this to himself for fear of sounding wimpish.

Robbie had been a Zodiac for just six months, having come down from Scotland. He had ended up in an unhealthy number of fights and made one too many enemies. He wanted a new start somewhere else, so he left his native land, headed south, and travelled down until he reached the sea.

So, he moved way down south to Griffton. However, he could not hold down a permanent job because he couldn't read or write well. That was when he found the Zodiacs. Of course, they made fun of his lazy eye but were very welcoming. They understood him. They knew he needed to escape his former life: his old adversaries and his mother who beat him. With the Zodiacs, he found acceptance and purpose.

They let him sleep at the warehouse along with a few others who didn't still live at home. It was fine because he had a sponge mat, a sleeping bag, and company. They ate together and stole together. It was much better than being alone.

Sometimes, Robbie was one of the ones who had to do the dirty work. He didn't mind this so much because it gave him some sort of respect from the others. But until now, he'd never killed anyone. They all knew this was expected of this job: no one had any delusions. There was a rumour amongst the boys, though, that there were women and children in the house. Although nobody said it out loud, they weren't looking forward to that part.

But they were Zodiacs, and they did whatever they had to do to get the job done and pick up their cash or take their spoil. Zodiacs were like pirates or highway robbers of old. Robbie sighed to himself, his eyes unfocused as he gazed into the distance at the house.

"Easy peasy," hissed Robbie over his right shoulder. He climbed back down from Toby's shoulders and pulled off his balaclava, revealing thick, curly black hair and a lazy eye.

All in all, the reconnaissance of the outer fence had been a success. There were no surprises so far. They had good news to report back to the boss, which was always a good thing.

DANIEL HAD WOKEN his wife and children, Rachel and Micah. They were now fully dressed, albeit alarmed by the news of the attack. The first thing he did was give them some sugary biscuits. The boys enjoyed this the most because it was like a midnight feast, and they giggled and nudged each other in the parlour where they were gathered.

"I've checked again, and there are some people outside, nosing around. They look like professional burglars, but I suspect there may be more to it, so I've activated a deterrent system I devised myself. Arabella knows about it. There is nothing to be alarmed about, if you'll pardon the pun. But if these people successfully evade my security, we need to be ready to move. Boys, get your rucksacks. Quickly pack three small toys each, a book to read, your handheld computers, and the clothes and toiletries Mama gives you. Micah, you know what to do. Rachel, are you okay? Good. Above all, don't be afraid; the Dunamis is with us." Rachel had gone from being bleary-eyed to fully awake. She looked over at Micah, who was stunningly handsome, even in the middle of the night.

"Shouldn't we call the police?" asked Rachel.

Daniel replied, "I don't think we'll be troubling them tonight. Right, everyone, it's time for the games. Everyone follow me." They all trailed to his study with Rachel at the rear.

She was puzzled by what he had said about games. She thought it was a rather strange thing to say.

MEANWHILE, the second group of Zodiacs had attempted to explore the back of the house. They quickly found they didn't have good access because the fence was too high to scale with their equipment.

Instead, they would have to approach it from the sides and the front as best they could. Then, they would have to cross the fields to the wall and climb into the inner core of the estate. The lads chose Doggo to tell Stevie the bad news.

~ 12345 ~

STEVIE LED THE ATTACK HIMSELF. He had learned from his scouts that the outer fences were some distance from the house. Between them and their target was a lower wall, easier to scale with a boost. Beyond that lay two or three large square gardens and the long driveway leading to the front of the house.

Stevie had an air rifle, knife, hammer, and flashlight in his backpack. He pulled on his fingerless gloves and balaclava and ordered Pig to help him up the fence.

"Do you know what, Pig? The thing I am looking forward to the most is gutting someone with my new blade." Pig snorted and grinned.

Then Stevie ascended the rope, throwing it over the metal fence and securing it tightly with a knot.

Further along, Robbie pulled himself up, hauled his body over the top of the high metal fence, and landed on top of a hedge. He scrambled down and landed on soft grass, smiling at the fact he hadn't broken or even twisted his ankles.

He felt the wetness of the ground beneath. The fields smelt of evergreens, mud, and grass. Long clouds above were streaked with moonlight, and the moon shone intensely in an otherwise black summer sky. It illuminated the fields that sloped up gently to the house and its walled garden. If the moon was the only thing watching them, they were in for an easy ride.

Toby landed beside Robbie. They paused and looked

around, listening hard. Down the line, other Zodiacs were touching down on the inside. They were a troupe of formidable figures dressed in black from head to toe.

All was quiet inside the estate grounds, and there were no indications of movement and no horses or cattle in sight.

Toby whispered, "What are you using? When it comes to finishing the job, I mean?"

But Robbie hadn't actually visualised killing anyone. If Stevie or Pig stood over him, he imagined he would have to do it. A bitter taste came into his mouth.

"Baseball bat. I've got a baseball bat in my bag," he whispered. "How about you?"

"A knife. I kept one of those Bowie knives that traitor Emerson was juggling. It's got a nice sharp blade. If I ever run into him again, he'll find out just how sharp it is."

"Yeah."

Then, the order came down the line: it was time to move forward. Everyone ran through the grounds, trying to make as little noise as possible. But the sound of two dozen young men tramping across a field with their great big boots was not a silent affair.

Halfway to the wall, they were arrested by the sound of a personal address system. It sounded like a loud air-raid siren that lasted for several seconds. The Zodiacs looked around them, confused. There was still no sign of anyone out in the open. Then, they heard a voice resonating through the air above their heads, which came from a series of speakers attached to the inner wall in the distance.

"This is a warning. You are trespassing on private property. Please leave immediately."

"Yeah, right," said Stevie Teeth sarcastically. "Just ignore it, boys. We move forward."

The voice carried on clearly, reminiscent of a train station announcement. "You are being observed on CCTV. Your movements are being recorded. This evidence will be handed to the police. Leave this property at once. You are trespassing on a private estate."

There was another pause. A few of the Zodiacs were reluctant to go on and had started to turn back and skulk away to the outer fence.

"Leave now, and you're dead," shouted Pig. "We're in this together. No one leaves. Everyone stays. They're just trying to scare us. But we don't scare easily. We're Zodiacs. Tell them down the line, we climb the wall, get in, and start smashing things up. No more messing about."

The disembodied voice rang out again. "This is your third and final warning. If you do not leave the premises immediately, we will not be liable for any injuries or loss of life that may ensue. You have been warned."

There was a period of silence longer than the previous ones.

Confident that the voice had been silenced, the Zodiac leader gave the order to assail the house one last time. He pulled out his knife and pointed it, blade forward, on the end of his outstretched arm.

"Come on lads. We're Zodiacs. No one tells us what to do," he shouted. "No one, ever. That's why we're Zodiacs."

With this and a handful of expletives, Stevie encouraged his gang to do what they were being paid to do. As one man, they ran across the bumpy ground to the wall. It was only five feet tall, maybe a little more, but for tall, strong young men, it posed no issue at all.

CHAPTER 22

Pig was a big guy, but even he felt the electric shock at the top of the wall when he pressed both hands down to vault over. He growled in pain.

"Yow!" said Robbie with a frown. Other Zodiacs were zapped by the thin web of electrified mesh over the brickwork. The top of the wall was an area of thirty centimetres in width. Only Stevie could hop up because he worked out quickly what was happening and used his sleeved forearms to shield him.

"Use your sleeves, lads," he hissed. "Once you're up, you're fine. It only seems to work on skin."

Gang members grunted in acknowledgment and were soon on top of the wall. Most of them spent little time up there and leapt quickly into the garden, except for Stevie. He wanted to see what was in store for them next. It didn't take long to find out.

Two Zodiacs went down, stumbling and falling into a deep pit. One of them was Robbie, who had twisted his ankle. The other was Tes.

"Are you two clowns all right?" Stevie called down from the wall.

"There's a hole down here. We fell in a hole," whined Robbie in his soft Glaswegian accent.

"We fell in a hole," imitated Stevie in a nasal whine. "Well, climb out, and let's get going!"

Tes pointed his flashlight at something in the pit and jabbered, "You need to see this. This sign says something about snakes."

"Snakes?" shrieked Robbie. "What sort of snakes?" "How should I know?"

"Read the sign." Robbie had a tinge of panic in his voice. "Just read it."

By now, Stevie had jumped down and stood at the pit's edge, leaning over. The other Zodiacs had gone ahead and were traipsing across the gardens. Some of them were heading for the Elizabethan gatehouse, the brick structure at the centre of the driveway that looked like a castle.

Unlike Robbie, Tes could read quite well. He followed the text with his finger, reading aloud and stumbling over the trickier words. "It says there are four types of snake poison. Cytotoxic venom has a localised action and affects the site of the bite. Proteolytic venom dismantles the molecular structure of the area surrounding and including the bite. Haemotoxic venoms act on the heart and cardiovascular system. Neurotoxic venom acts on the nervous system and brain. That's all it says."

Tes quickly shone his torch around their feet, flashing it into the corners. He could see twigs, mud, and leaves. There were plenty of places for snakes to hide. Stevie was also pointing his flashlight in every direction, looking for anything that moved. Robbie and Tes climbed out of the hole speedily, jabbering warnings to the other gang members.

Almost immediately, a set of floodlights came on. The roof-mounted halogen bulbs were accompanied by wailing sirens. The deafening volume of noise seemed to come from every-where. Startled and scared, a good number of Zodiacs threw themselves back over the wall. They were shocked by the mesh again but continued to race away from the estate.

"Cowards," shouted Stevie. "I'll find out who you are and bite your ears off."

Then, to Pig, he called, "Pig, where are you? Let's get this thing done. Lads, there are no snakes here. It's a trick. That makes me so angry."

❧ 12345 ❧

UNDER THE FLOODLIGHTS, the Zodiacs had a clear view of the grounds. They could see every shrub, hedge, plant pot, and garden ornament.

Toby led some of the Zodiacs to the gatehouse. They had broken down a door that led to a spiral staircase inside one of the four turrets. Floodlit from the house, they made their way easily to the top, which opened up to a parapet that gave them a good view over the estate.

Suddenly, Toby found himself under attack. Large bullets were being fired from the house. He heard the whizzing of flying projectiles and the splatting sound they made as they hit the walls.

Paintball bullets.

One of them smacked him in the neck, making him yowl. Ducking down, he cried out to his gang members to take cover. "They're firing at us!"

"We know," said one of his comrades. He watched the Zodiacs scatter down below as they took incoming fire from the main house.

The paintball tirade ceased just as quickly as it had started.

The public address system leapt to life. "This house is fully armed. You have been warned in the strongest terms to leave immediately. For your own safety, you are urged to cease trespassing and leave now."

This latest announcement spurred at least half a dozen young men to run for the five-foot wall that encircled the garden. It amounted to a rout when added to the number that had fled previously. Just Stevie, Pig, Robbie, Toby and some others remained. Robbie and Toby were in the tower, and the others were in the garden.

"Oh, come on. What's wrong with you? You're a bunch of cowards. There's no bullets and no snakes. The electric fence doesn't even work properly," screamed Stevie Teeth. "You're out, all of you. You're not Zodiacs anymore. You're nothing. I don't want you in the gang. So why don't you all run? Just make sure I don't catch up with you."

At that very moment, the sound of gunfire filled the air. It was eardrum-splitting, high-velocity, firecracker gunfire. Smoke erupted across the garden, leaving eerie clouds hanging in the air, caught in the floodlights.

Pig swore loudly. Stevie watched his fat frame jogging away. "Not you too, Pig. Is anyone still with me?"

But the other two in the garden had beaten Pig to the outer perimeter and were gone, up the ropes and over the top of the metal fence. There was another explosion halfway down the drive. As the echo died, Stevie yelled, "Shout out your names, whoever's left."

Robbie and Toby called out from the top of the tower as they began to make their way down. Toby was rubbing his neck from where he'd got shot. Robbie was coughing with the smoke. They emerged at the bottom of the gatehouse, looking forlorn. They had pulled their balaclavas off and were holding them in their hands. Robbie staggered forward and leaned his arm against the gnarly bark of an ancient elm tree. He stared into space.

The whole experience had been reminiscent of a time when he had been caught in the crossfire of two Glasgow gangs. He had been playing in the street at night when the two sides started hurling fireworks at each other. It was terrifying.

"Just the three of us, is it?" snarled Stevie. They could see his teeth through the slit in his balaclava.

"All right lads, we're beaten. Retreat. Just try not to get shot in the head on the way out. We've obviously walked into a trap. Someone's gonna pay for this."

⚬⚬ 12345 ⚬⚬

"IN THE PAST, my security systems would feature live rounds of ammo, with high-voltage electric fences, hunting dogs, that sort of thing. But these days, I don't get any pleasure from maiming or killing people," Daniel explained to Rachel.

"Oh, that's good."

They were all sitting in his study on the east side of the house so he could watch what was going on through his computer screens.

"One of my favourite bits is a snakepit down near the wall. I haven't actually got any snakes in there. We'd most likely lose them in the garden. Or they'd end up biting the kids. But I do have a great sign that lists the different ways that snakes can kill. I'm hoping our visitors had a good read of that."

"Are they gone?" asked Rory. He was holding a complex and colourful Lego model of a spaceship.

"I think so. But let me just check one last time." Daniel turned his head to his surveillance screens and started pressing buttons. Rachel looked around at his amazing study. The room had wood-panelled walls up to the ceiling. It also had a large open fireplace with a spectacular columned and carved chimney breast featuring a family coat of arms. Old books lined the walls, not paperbacks, but heavy hardbacks with gold lettering and faded red, blue, and green spines. The room had an aroma reminiscent of autumn walks through the woods.

Rachel had noted that the study was next to the breakfast room and kitchen at the back of the house. Beyond this lay the newer parts of the building, including the orangery and billiard room. She remembered it from her grand tour with Rory and Cameron. She had also learned that there was an ensuite bathroom adjoining the study, which was very unusual. To get to the grand reception hall at the front of the house, you had to walk past a stair column leading up on one side and down on the other.

Upstairs were bedrooms and dressing rooms. Downstairs, on the lower ground floor, the boys showed her the storerooms, laundry, boiler rooms, and another large kitchen. It had been a head-spinning experience. The house was so different from her dad's three-bedroom box.

"Hold on, everyone, we're not alone," said Daniel quickly. "Those kids have gone, but it looks like something else has arrived. Something worse."

☙ 12345 ❧

IT WAS AROUND two o'clock in the morning. No one in Griffton saw the Dream Fighters arrive. There were sixty of them, all dressed in black and brown leather garments. Long metal breastplates protected their fronts, and their sword hilts bobbed up and down at their waists as they marched. The men travelled in groups of six: ten groups marching in two-by-three formations. They moved swiftly and quietly down from Griffton Cliff. Dust rose from under their boots. Before long, they were on the main road.

In the distance, the city slept.

☙ 12345 ❧

"THEY'RE at the outer fence. Looks like scores of them – maybe even hundreds. I reckon we've got ten minutes max. We're moving to Plan B," Daniel informed everyone. He fiddled with his computers, deleting files and grabbing a few slim hard drives from a server rack beneath his desk. Meanwhile, he slung his rucksack on his back.

While he worked, he spoke rapidly, his words clipped and

short. "Plan B is we need to get out of here, and fast. Everyone grab your bags."

They heard a series of hard, loud knocks, then the shattering of glass at the front section of the house. Daniel glanced at his screen one last time before pressing a switch that killed the power. It looked to Rachel like they were under attack from armed men from medieval times.

"They're coming from the front of the house and the east and west sides. We need to leave the house quickly. Everyone over to the fire."

Daniel crouched before his Elizabethan fireplace, which had a wall of naked brickwork at the back. He lifted out the black metal log basket and set it aside.

"It's an old Priest's Hole," he said by way of explanation. He pulled up a massive slab of stone, hinged at the front, to reveal a set of steep wooden steps that led into darkness. "Everyone in, it's quite safe – Rachel first, then Bella and the boys." He handed Rachel and his wife torches. "It's okay, I have been down before. I'll close the hatch after us. From the outside, it just looks like an ordinary fireplace."

Then, they were on the move.

The escapees travelled down a long way before coming to a plateau with a dry mud base and brick sides. Rachel saw they were in a long arched tunnel that was, thankfully, relatively clear of cobwebs or debris. Daniel and Micah had to stoop as they walked, but the others could travel through easily without hitting their heads. Daniel had taken the lead with Micah close behind, shining his torch ahead of them. The further they went, the patchier the brickwork became, giving way to roughly hewn stone pieces encased in mud.

Daniel started to chat with Micah. "Caleb mentioned these guys. They're called Dream Fighters. They have devoted their lives to following Samyaza, and you can be sure that wherever they gather, nothing good happens. I am confident we can beat them with the help of the Dunamis, but for the time being, this seems the best option. I just hope they won't destroy our house."

Then he called behind him, "How are my brave soldiers? All okay?" Rachel and Arabella had Cameron and Rory between them, who nodded and smiled with flushed faces.

The tunnel concluded in a flight of steps that led upward to another trapdoor, which Daniel confidently pushed open, drawing in a rush of clean night air. They emerged somewhere in the broad forest that encircled the back of the estate. All around them was darkness.

Daniel searched around with the beam of his flashlight and noticed that Arabella was weeping silently. He grabbed her hand. In the distance, they could hear the security sirens sounding over their home, an undulating air-raid wail. The Dream Fighters had broken in and taken over the mansion in a bloodless coup. Their master, Samyaza, would be pleased, Daniel thought.

CHAPTER 23

Caleb, Eli, and Anton were forced to walk out of the farmhouse and down the path around the village. It was a beautiful day. Onlookers may have mistaken the party for a group of three men travelling together for the fun of it. But at their backs were the two big warriors and the pair of young teenagers.

It did give the friends time to catch up, however. Their captors had also allowed each swig of water and a couple of dry cakes so their most basic needs were met.

"Bolivia is a spectacular place," Caleb said. He told them about his journey from Santa Cruz into the semi-tropical lush green countryside and farming territories.

The men walked along a dirt track surrounded by wild greenery. Built for adventure, they admired the creation around them, from the tiny insects to the massive trees.

"So, Anton, tell me about your Peregrine Falcon. The one in the cage in your garden shed. We let him out, by the way."

"Excellent! Thank you! Yes, Edgar injured his wing, and the authorities let me keep him. I nursed him back to health. They're such powerful birds, don't you think?"

"When I lived in Israel, I kept birds," said Eli. "But nothing as big as a falcon. I liked the little tropical ones. Their chatter was amusing. There's nothing quite like a conversation between birds."

"Do you remember those rare birds we saw in the Vršac Mountains in Vojvodina?"

"That was a treat," replied Eli. "A short-toed eagle and a Honey Buzzard."

"Very rare. Wonderful," said Anton rapturously. "There were also meant to be Rock Buntings, but they are so hard to find. We never got to see any."

"I do love the mountains. We were very high up then. In the heights, the view is out of this world," said Eli. Then he called backwards to the two boys and spoke in Spanish, "So, what's your story? How did you get to join these bandits?"

Diego piped up, "They're not bandits. These are our friends. They rescued us from bad men."

José nudged him and shook his head. "You shouldn't speak to them," he whispered.

Eli interjected, "It's okay. We are not armed. Do we look dangerous to you? A bunch of old men? No, we are friendly. So, tell me, these men came out of nowhere, correct? They drove out your enemies?"

Diego was nodding. Fortunately, the two Dream Fighters either seemed unaware or didn't feel any need to interrupt conversations, especially those in Spanish. They had set their faces and were looking forward, beyond the men and into the distance. They had their job to do, perhaps an execution, and nothing else seemed to matter.

Emboldened, Eli continued, "Just because they rescued you from your enemies doesn't mean that they are not the enemy themselves."

José said to Diego, "These men are trying to trick us. We know these warriors are our friends. Papa is convinced. They have looked after us. They have trained us. There must be a reason these three men cannot be trusted."

Diego's face hardened, and he nodded and blinked at his brother. After that, the two boys marched behind the Dream Fighters, using them as a barrier. The conversation was over.

❧ 12345 ❧

"BUT I DON'T UNDERSTAND," said Benson loudly. "I thought I was useful to you. I know you're not the beautiful angel I thought you were, the one you pretended to be. The one I fell in love with. I understand. I know all about lying and tricks. But I forgive you. And I'm still happy to work with you – to be partners."

"Well, bully for you," snarled Samyaza somewhere inside Benson Steel's personage.

"You really helped me. And I do appreciate it. I mean, obviously, my business empire was all me. I was the one who worked hard and built it up. But the past few months I've known you, even how you look now, has been useful to me. You helped me understand how I can use my skills to get results. And what you showed me, the things in the heavenly realms, and the things coming in the future. They're unbelievable! I want to be part of it."

"Oh blah, blah, blah, do stop going on. The truth, Mr Steel, is you and I have now come to the end of the road. Like I said before, the problem is I really don't like you. Okay, I love the fact that you lie, steal, hurt people, and do whatever it takes. But as far as humans go, you really are the worst kind. *Comprende?* I hate you with a passion."

"I can change. What do you need me to do?" Benson had his hand on his chest, and the strangest feeling there was a face inside him that was trying to get out through his skin. He was standing alone in his office at night: his tall tower that overlooked Griffton City. It was the early hours of the morning, and the assault on Daniel's mansion was complete.

"I don't care that I gave you a series of tasks to accomplish, and you executed them poorly. Actually, I tell a lie. I do care. I asked you to kill the girl, and you didn't do it. I asked you to get your teenagers to kill my enemies. They didn't. Now, I've had to bring in outside help. Hopefully, they will finish the job. But you're out of the loop now."

Benson Steel stared at his framed pictures, his executive table and chair, and the tiny bits of desk clutter that provide a working environment, which were the essential fragments of his life.

"But you need me." His voice wavered.

Somehow, Samyaza had got hold of his arms and legs and moved him over to the window.

"What are you going to do?"

"It's time to find someone with a backbone. And it's time for me to be free again. Free to work with someone who's really hungry for action. Someone younger and fitter, for sure."

Benson watched his hands fiddle with the latch and open the window. It was just big enough for a body to squeeze through, but it took some effort because of his bulging stomach and chest.

"Benson, Benson. I do wish you'd worked a bit harder at the gym", chided Samyaza.

⤜ 12345 ⤛

DANIEL LED his family through the forest with the sound of the sirens at their backs.

"Mind your footing there," he warned every so often.

Rachel was glad she had her trainers on, and the girls hadn't minded her wearing them to work at Nightshift. She generally dressed up for the publishing house but hadn't felt like it when she went in yesterday. She felt twigs crunch underfoot, and her rucksack was heavy on her back. They had given her the bag to help distribute their possessions, and she seemed to carry some bulky items.

The forest was made up of broad-leaved trees with branches that formed a natural canopy, and the flashlights were vital for seeing the way ahead.

Rachel thought the young boys, Cameron and Rory, were so brave. It helped her to keep going. She did sniff every so often, though, fighting back her tears. She wondered about Lake, Iona, and her life down in Griffton. She worried about the Initiation and the bad things that were happening, orchestrated by Samyaza. There was a feeling of dread and even self-hatred at the thought that she had considered joining him.

In the pit of her stomach, she was also experiencing the same feelings she had gone through last year. Yes, she enjoyed the thrill of the adventure a bit, but she also felt under attack and hopeless. It was a cocktail of emotions. But this changed as she listened to the boys.

They sang a quiet song as they went. Once in a while, they forgot some of the words and told each other to start from the beginning. But it lifted her spirits and gave her a sense of hope. Something deep inside her assured her that life had changed radically for the better. In fact, it would never be the same again. She felt inexpressible joy welling up in her heart, elation that brought tears to her eyes.

After a while, Daniel got everyone to pause in a clearing in the forest where the moon shone down and lit up the children's faces. "This is where we're going to stop to catch our breath." Micah handed out a couple of bottles of water, which they shared.

Looking at Rachel, Daniel said, "You know he's with us, don't you?"

"What do you mean?"

"I can see it. You are calm, and your heart feels warm, doesn't it? You feel joy, though the situation we face is uncertain. Am I right?"

"Yes. It's the Dunamis, isn't it?"

Daniel and Arabella nodded in unison, and Rachel saw

Micah smile under the torchlight. Arabella closed her eyes and relaxed. Daniel added, "That means the Rescuer is fighting for us in the heavenly realms. Every minute, he's winning victories against our hidden enemies who would do us harm."

"You guys are so strange," said Rachel. "But in a good way. And I want what you've got." And in her head, she said, "I'm tired of being scared and alone, a little girl sitting in the dark."

Daniel cocked his head to one side, like a rabbit hearing a distant foe.

"We'd better get going. Let's stay ahead of the Dream Fighters." They took up their rucksacks and resumed their trek.

Rachel scrambled through twigs and undergrowth again. Her body was feeling very cold. She was used to being asleep at this time. Her face was icy, and she shook from fatigue. She wondered how on earth the young boys found the energy to keep up the pace. Several times, she leaned heavily on the rough bark of a fir tree to steady her. Her legs had started to ache, but still, they pressed on. She had never explored the forests around Griffton before, and this was the reason.

They came to a coppice, an area of woodland that had been cut back to ground level. There were piles of firewood nearby, and Daniel led them through the clearing, informing them they'd reached the edge of a farm that bordered the woods. They left the forest and entered a field, with the starry night sky affording them all the light they needed to see.

"If I know John Bosworth, I know he'll have his tractor somewhere in one of these fields."

Minutes later, they had located the farmer's tractor, which still had the keys in it, as was common practice with farm vehicles in remote places. "I'm sure John won't mind us borrowing this," Daniel told his children as everyone climbed aboard. "After all, it is an emergency."

The throaty diesel engine sparked to life.

THE PLAN WAS to drive out of the field, find the main road, and take Rachel home because she had had enough adventure for one night. Daniel also thought it would be a good idea to head for the city and find help or a mobile phone signal at the very least.

However, one field seemed to lead to another, and before long, they were lost. More importantly, the tractor ran out of fuel, leaving them stranded on a steep incline. There was a slightly tense atmosphere between Daniel and Arabella, but Rachel saw her yield to his leadership as he said they would continue on foot, climbing up the slope. "There's not much to see behind us, but we might get a better view of where we are if we keep going up."

"I also sense it is the right thing to do. The Dunamis is leading us that way," Micah agreed.

Rachel was reminded of her hair-raising trip up to Lower Ledge Crossing when she saw the lights that miraculously deposited her on the beach last summer.

Although it was slow going, Micah checked on Rachel now and then, which she liked. Soon, it became apparent they were ascending Griffton Cliff from the west. Before long, they found themselves at the top of the cliff with its panoramic view across the ocean and the city below them.

Rachel gave a sigh of relief now that she had rediscovered her bearings. The sea was magnificent at night. She had always loved seeing it under clear midnight skies.

The wind up here was even colder, and it whipped them mercilessly. Micah held her arm tenderly and stood by her. "Are you okay, Rachel?" he asked. She loved the way he said her name, this supernaturally handsome man whom she had met just yesterday. It made her melt inside.

"Yes, I think so," she breathed. Her heart was doing somersaults again. Why couldn't it be like this with Lake? Lake was sweet, with his floppy brown hair and overactive sense of humour. Sometimes, it felt like he tried too hard. On the other hand, sometimes it felt like he didn't try at all. But what was missing between her and Lake was this almost tangible thrill that ran like an electric current between them.

Micah's hand quickly disappeared from her arm as if he had read her thoughts. They turned to see Daniel's family huddling together, the four of them sharing a hug.

Micah turned to Rachel again. "They're really an amazing family."

"They certainly have something." Rachel smiled.

She added, "I can't believe what happened to their house – the windows getting smashed like that, and all those men everywhere. But it's your home too, isn't it, that amazing building? You all took it so well. What on earth happened back there?" She stared into the valley, trying to make out the mansion estate. But from where she was standing, all she could see were the tops of the trees in the moonlight.

"Sacrifice in a word. Our enemy prowls around like a roaring lion, looking for someone to devour. We must be prepared to make sacrifices if we insist on opposing him and following the Rescuer and his Dunamis."

"Sacrifice?" mused Rachel. She thought of all the things she had lost in her life. She counted her mother, her father, and her finger. Then she thought of her best friend Lara, Iona – almost – and Lake to some extent, and even her very normality. "Sacrifice," she said again, speaking the word into the wind.

"But that's not the end of it," said Micah sweetly. "Sometimes we need to experience sacrifice so we can gain something even better, beyond our dreams. There comes a point when you have to lay down your life to gain it afresh."

In the far distance, along the edge of the cliff, she spied the stone head.

"Look. Over there," she shouted out. "It's that head. It's the stone carving from the newspaper."

"So it is," said Daniel. "Come on, let's have a closer look."

CHAPTER 24

The journey had been just the right length for the three friends to catch up with each other. They chatted away nonchalantly, striding ahead of their captors, who could just as well have been on an expedition of their own.

They looked an interesting group of men as they walked up and down the hills. Somebody might have viewed them as a father with his two sons were it not for the fact that they looked so different from each other. There was Caleb with his tightly cropped hair, round black sunglasses, strong shoulders, and muscular arms. He laughed freely and walked tall. His steps were light but confident. Next to him was the slimmer and taller Anton. He laughed less frequently and made wry observations as they went. Anton was a little faded and a bit unkempt. He could be the older brother.

Third was Eli, the sprightly septuagenarian with long, wavy grey-white hair. For him, everything was exciting and interesting, worthy of observation and comment. He watched everything closely and keenly; you could almost see his brain running complex analytical algorithms.

And so, they walked on through the morning, prisoners of

the silent Dream Fighters and the two young boys, not that anyone would have guessed.

When the stone head appeared in the distance on a hill, Eli raised his eyebrows. He gave Caleb a look, and Caleb nodded back. Anton was the only one who didn't register any emotion, though he looked keenly at the obelisk.

The lump of carved rock eyed them impassively. It seemed to say to them, "None shall pass." Their only option was to go around it. This was not, however, the Dream Fighters' intention.

It was taller than any of them. It rose about ten feet high with eyes set deep in, presumably made with some sort of long chisel. Above the eyeholes was a wide brow, and below was a wide frog-like mouth. Fashioned from some kind of smooth, light grey stone, the head sat heavily on a thick neck with the hill beneath. The bright sunlight fell on it, showing up every ridge and fissure.

They could hear a dull hum emanating from the stone head. "You people really know how to get ahead," said Eli. "Get ahead, get a head – it's meant to be a joke. Do any of you have a sense of humour?"

Anton was shaking his head, his eyes sparkling.

In response, one of the Dream Fighters said, "Enough talk. You boys. Come. You will like this."

"We know this head," said José. "But it's not good to touch it. You ask Diego here. Something happened to him. Something bad."

Diego stayed quiet and kept his distance from the monolith.

Without further ado, one Dream Fighter grabbed hold of Eli with both hands on his bony shoulders. The other manhandled Anton. They led them up the hill.

Before them towered the broad stone head. It stared at them all the while.

"No," gasped Diego. "It will kill them."

The warriors threw Anton and Eli with an incredible amount

of force at the stone head. Unable to resist, they went headlong towards it. At the point of impact, with an audible hiss of static, the men fell into the huge face and disappeared from sight. It was almost as though they had been dropped into water and sunk to the bottom, except there were no ripples in the smooth stone.

José and Diego stared, rooted to the spot. Then, the men rounded on Caleb, each taking hold of one arm.

⁓ 12345 ⁓

Serena was in St Malo in northern France. She had been sent by the angel in New York to an appointment with someone or something. She didn't know for sure. She still felt sad about leaving Caleb at the airport, which she knew was probably silly. She had only met him twice now, but there was a strong bond between them into which the Dunamis seemed to breathe life. She desperately hoped Caleb was well, and his trip to Bolivia was going all right, but she hadn't heard anything from him or the Dunamis, which was hard to bear. The angel had told her she would know how to contact him at the right time, and she had no option but to trust that this would be the case.

Brittany, this northwestern slice of France, was beautiful in the summer. It was so ancient and attractive. She looked out to sea as she walked along the walls of the small, coastal fortress city. The water had a deep blue hue, and birds hopped onto the gentle waves and soared into the distance. She inhaled the smell of clean sea air.

Serena stopped by a heavy grey canon, weathered, worn, and stationed on a wooden cart. It was covered with red, chipped paint through which the wood could be seen. A clock chimed down within the walled port city.

She leaned on the sea-facing wall made of great rectangular blocks of stone. Out to sea was a little grassy-topped island and a smaller island with a fort that made it look like a top hat.

Serena felt a momentary twang of pain, but it wasn't in her body. It was deep down in her spirit. The Dunamis had shown, in a split second, that everything was not okay with Caleb. Her adrenalin pumped with the new information, and she went into immediate intercession, fighting in the spiritual realms for Caleb's safety and wellbeing.

A group of tourists, men, women, and children, bustled past her. They pointed out to the sea, chattering excitedly and moving quickly. Serena remained static, a solitary, leaning figure with long wavy hair, bleached blonde by the Indonesian sun.

If anyone paid closer attention to her, they would notice her eyes were screwed shut, and her hand was pressed against her heart. Her dress whipped about her as the wind caught the seam, like the boats that rushed by with their sails unfurled.

The prophetess had a vision of a strong and muscular figure. He was curled into a ball on the ground, bowed down and subdued in a thick purple fog, unable to move, unable to speak, wholly and utterly defeated.

"Oh, Caleb," she sighed desperately. "Oh, my Caleb."

⟡ 12345 ⟡

"HE LOOKS LIKE A GRUMPY MAN," commented Rory. They stood around the stone head on the top of Griffton Cliff.

"Remember not to touch, boys," Daniel reminded them. The boys danced around the monolithic structure. They circled it several times, pumped with prepubescent energy. The moon and stars gave them enough light to see the way and keep clear of the edge that dropped away into the coastal city of Griffton.

"I think he fell from interplanetary space," said Cameron. "That's what I think." He had a knowing look, and his big, saucer-like eyes glowed.

"Don't be silly. Someone put him there. It's like a joke. Not actually a joke, but like a joke," said Rory.

Daniel and Arabella stood and marvelled at it. Meanwhile,

Micah was trying to get a signal on his mobile phone. Rachel herself had had enough of cross-country hiking for the time being. She was glad to be out of the forest.

The exhilaration of getting free from their attackers had worn off. She had now witnessed the stone head for herself and could tick that one off the list. But she was tired now, and it was time to switch off. She was perfectly happy to sit down on the grass and do nothing except stare out over the cliff. She pulled her jacket up to her neck to keep warm. Somewhere down there was Griffton Hospital, where her friend Iona lay recovering in her bed. Lake was down there, too. He was probably sound asleep in his bed. She had no clue what her dad was up to or whether he was even home.

Right now, home was an abstract concept, something that felt very distant. It was a place where she kept her clothes, her books, and her stuff. It was a place of terrible memories and long hours of crying.

But now she had found this happy, strange, exciting family, and they had welcomed her in. She had also found Micah and the world seemed to be a better place. Perhaps that was what he meant by sacrifice. You lose something, maybe everything, so you can gain something better.

Was Micah the something better? She was wary of trusting her emotions because she so often got it wrong. She knew deep down that she had been right not to trust Samyaza, even though she had been tempted by his proposal. It was a trap. She knew things would have gone from bad to worse if she had sided with him. Yes, she would have been on the side that was winning at the moment, but it clearly would have meant destroying this lovely family.

"Daniel. The Dream Fighters are here," yelled Micah. In the distance, half a dozen warriors had appeared. Rachel gasped. She had never seen anything like it. She knew about Storm Troopers from Star Wars. She was familiar with Vikings from school history. But these men looked fiercer and rougher than any fighting men she had seen on television. And they were coming to get her.

On one side of them lay a perilous drop; on the other, the open fields rolled away to the north. They could continue along the edge of the cliff, which led to a long, curvy road back down to Lower Ledge Crossing and into Griffton. But if they took that route, they were sure to be outrun.

Suddenly, the children made the decision for them. Rory saw the warriors coming and bolted toward the stone head. He stumbled on a clump of grass, tripped toward the structure, and fell headlong into it. As he did so, he just sort of slipped in, Rachel observed in alarm.

The sound of Arabella screaming filled her ears.

Cameron raced after his brother, running at the stone head like an open doorway. He was calling for his brother but was silenced mid-cry as he, too, disappeared into the sculpture.

Arabella rushed towards the megalith with her arms outstretched. As she laid her palms on its surface, she fell forward. Rachel and the two men helplessly watched her go.

Daniel took one look behind his shoulder. The men were now trotting towards them. He looked at Micah, glanced at the stone head, closed his eyes for a moment, and then plunged forward. Micah followed him, a true and faithful servant to the last, without hesitating.

Reeling from the mind-bending scene she had just witnessed, Rachel stood at the edge of the cliff, all alone. She stared like a rabbit transfixed by a set of vehicle headlights.

She could now clearly see that the six men wore leather and brass armour. They looked like seasoned soldiers, men who were used to battle. Their helmets covered their heads, but she could see their faces, which were weather-worn and scarred, unshaven but focused, and they were coming for her.

The soldiers covered the distance quickly, narrowing Rachel's options down. She could move towards them with her arms up and get captured or killed. Alternatively, she could leap off the cliff and end it all. Or she could follow Micah and the Harcourt family into the unknown. She could pass into the stone head, the giant structure made of solid, impenetrable rock.

Rachel decided, took a deep breath, and sprinted headlong into the stone statue.

CHAPTER 25

Some people knew this land as Elysium, or perhaps the Elysian Fields, after which the Avenue des Champs-Élysées in Paris was named. Others called it the Underworld or Place of the Dead. The Sapana had their own name for it, which meant the place of Dreams, hence their name, the Sapana 'Dream' Fighters.

Regardless of the name, Caleb sat dreaming in this place. He was a pilot once again, flying a Boeing 787 Dreamliner, an aircraft he'd never flown and was likely never to fly. Somewhere over the Pacific, his vehicle had developed an engine fault and caught fire. He was thirty-seven thousand feet up and in charge of a fully laden passenger plane. It turned into a fireball as the people screamed. He was the last to die.

In his next dream, Caleb was hiking in the mountains. He was somewhere in Eastern Europe, climbing alone. As he stepped off a ledge, his foot got caught in a tight, rocky hole. It held firm like a limpet, and his body convulsed with the pain of a broken ankle.

An ice storm blew up around him, and he could not move his foot, so he was forced to sit down. It was so cold. Eventually, crushed by snow, Caleb froze to death.

It was blisteringly hot now. A score of angry scorpions approached his parched body in a desert, and he realised he was in the next dream. He was lost amidst the sand dunes, which rose in semicircular peaks around him. He was somewhere near Jordan. He could make out the sharp ridges but squinted as the scorching sun reflected off the sand. The backs of his eyes burned.

Death by scorpion was a slow process, and the fall from this dream was a long and painful spiral down to the bottom.

He dreamt of his lovely and loyal wife, Rosemarie. She was standing in their kitchen, her long, straight hair around her shoulders. Her slow death had had a profound effect on him. Seeing her again, even in this endless dream world, was difficult. She was so real. When she spoke and said his name, it was as though she had never left him.

But in this terrible dream, his dear wife Rosemarie informed him she had been seeing another man. She had been romantically involved with Anton, whom he loved as a brother. The sense of betrayal seared his heart, though his brain reminded him this was just an illusion.

Caleb sat on the cold ground, hunched into a ball, his forearms against his forehead and his fingers on his crown. Beside him, Eli and Anton sat in their own personal netherworld. Three bulbous sacks sat heavily on the tops of their heads, bobbing gently. Around the three of them, the purple mists swelled. A stifling, leathery stench filled the Elysian air.

Caleb moaned, but no one heard him except for the Creator, the Rescuer, and their Dunamis. They knew such things must happen for a time but that nothing happens without a reason. With compassion, they watched their warriors.

⤳ 12345 ⤳

A HOMELESS WOMAN found Benson's body as she drifted through the streets after a sleepless night in a doorway. The businessman was lying at an awkward angle at the foot of his office block. His glasses were several feet away, and one of the lenses was shattered. His smartphone was also in several pieces. It had a smashed screen and a mangled memory card that was no longer readable. The memory card had been the only place that held the CCTV footage of Rachel in the Griffton Metropolitan Hotel.

The rough sleeper bent over, feeling the ache in her back and side. She turned the phone with her fingernails but eventually walked away.

The second person who found Benson's body was someone in his human resources department, coming in early to work. She gasped when she saw him but didn't scream.

She phoned the police only when she had made a coffee and took it to her desk.

⌒⁓ 12345 ⁓⌒

"THERE'S something you need to know about Rachel," Kumi informed Lake.

Lake still wasn't a hundred percent clear how she had ended up at his house and was accompanying him on his walk to work from the east side of the city centre. But she was beautiful and had a short pink skirt, long legs, and a purple flower in her hair, and he liked all of these things. He also liked how she stared intensely into his eyes, catlike, when she spoke to him and how she smelled of flowers and danger.

"Hold on a minute. I thought you didn't know Rachel. So, now you're telling me you do know her?" he quizzed her as they walked.

"Oh yeah. We grew up together. But we kind of fell out. We don't like to talk about it. I know her really well, though, like a sister, in fact."

Lake looked sidelong at her. "Really? You're kidding me."

"Sure. We used to play dolls together and everything."

"I had no idea. So, what is it you think I need to know about Rachel? Should I get my notebook out and take notes?"

Kumi smirked and leered at Lake, saying, "No, you don't have to get anything out."

"So?"

"She's gone away for a bit."

"What? How do you know? You said you fell out with her."

"I keep in touch with her now and again. Anyway, she wanted me to give you this."

She handed an envelope to Lake. It was a printed letter, which Lake thought was a bit formal for Rachel.

It read, "Dear Lake, I've taken some time off work, and I'm going away for a bit to stay with my family in Birmingham. Things aren't really working out between us, and to be honest, there is no more 'you and me.' I know you know what I'm talking about. Anyway, I'd rather you didn't try to call me. But I'm sure I'll see you around. By the way, things went fine up at the house. There's nothing to worry about anymore, and it's all cool now. Well, take care. Rachel."

Lake stared at the letter, re-read it, and absent-mindedly plunged it into his pocket.

"I don't believe it," he commented quietly. Then he locked his eyes on the pavement.

They walked silently for a while, crossed a road together, and came to Roasting Vale Lane, the main road that ran along the east side of the city centre. Lake looked like a wounded animal.

"We both know she has issues. But, you know, sometimes you need to lose something to gain something better. Do you know what I mean, Lakie?" She clasped his hand and pulled him towards her. He could smell her perfume, like a bouquet of spring flowers.

"Don't you think it's destiny that we met up, and at exactly the time when Rachel realises she has to move on?"

Lake stifled a sob which had crept up on him by hiding in

his throat. The depth of emotion he felt for Rachel hit him like a baseball bat on the back of his head.

Rachel's huge brown eyes and so many memories of the past year surfaced in his mind. He thought about the times they had shared on the cliff and beach. Admittedly, most of those times had been last summer, but he really thought they had something. But, if he was honest with himself, she had been hard work. Kumi had voiced his major concern, which was that she had issues. She just wasn't easy company. Kumi was so right.

"I mean, obviously, things take time. But I want you to know I'm here for you, Lake. And I'm not going anywhere." She smiled at him, a big-lipped, big-eyed, warm, and embracing smile that felt like a blowtorch blasting at the icicles around his heart. They walked without talking, just looking ahead of them,

Kumi and Lake.

In her spirit, her handsome, brown surfer dude winked at her, his curly black hair tumbling around his ocean-wet hair. She knew he wasn't a real person, as human beings are real people. But he enchanted her and entranced her. He wooed her soul with his rich, deep, booming voice and masculine charm. He offered her wicked adventure and illicit intimacy. It was the pull of the darkness, the thrill of the wrong.

Then she felt her internal organs turn to marshmallows again as Samyaza said to her, "I am so proud of you, my darling Kumiko. The boy has no idea, and you played your part expertly. You have spun your web, and he is trapped like a fly. So have some fun. Have some fun, dearest Kumi. There is a lot of work ahead of us, but I trust you will find it as enjoyable as this assignment. After you say your goodbyes, head back up to the mansion. There are Sapanas and others to instruct, and they await your orders, General Kumiko. But don't worry, I'll tell you what to say."

"Mmm," said Kumi audibly.

"I'm sorry?"

"Oh, I was just enjoying your company," lied Kumi.

Lake smiled. In the distance, he saw the Griffton News Tower. He could glimpse, through the high windows, the early morning shift of reporters. They were tapping out the breaking news and getting their quotes by phone. Right up at the top was where the executives would gather to forge their strategy later in the day. On the floors below, the sales teams were already in, keeping the wheels of the paper rolling as they sold their ads.

Then, lower still, production and subeditors would meet to bring Lake's text to life. Deliveries and distribution took place on the lower ground levels. It was Lake's paper where he felt most at home. Rachel had left him, but he was content to go to work and try to forget.

Forget Rachel Race.

"This is where I say bye-bye for now," said Kumi. "But I'll come check on you later, okay?"

"Okay," replied Lake, grasping the lifeline. He allowed her to kiss him goodbye.

CHAPTER 26

They gathered in the ground floor drawing room of Lytescote Manor. Three top city councillors, the Chief of Police, the publisher of the Griffton News, and the heads of several of Griffton's leading businesses. There were others, too, such as men and women in their middle years or older. Some of them were acquainted with each other, and some were not. They sat in their places, on a sofa or a chair, surrounded by a ring of Dream Fighters.

The light in the room was dull, and muffled thuds could be heard in other parts of the house.

"But you're just a young whippersnapper," complained an elderly gentleman in a grey suit and dark blue waistcoat. He sat at the centre of a row of upright chairs with his hands on a mahogany walking stick. It had a horse's head and a gilt collar.

"Appearances can be deceptive," replied Kumi in a disarmingly girly voice. "You need to know I have the power and authority of Master Samyaza. Many of us here know him and serve him. Do you really think the Sapanas would listen to me if I didn't? Course not."

There was murmuring amongst the group as they looked at the fierce warriors who lined the edge of the Persian rug.

"So, if anyone has a problem taking instructions from a girl, my Dream Fighters will be happy to take you out."

No one moved. The old man bristled but stayed in his place, clutching his cane even tighter.

"Good, then we can move on. We all have our interests to protect, so naturally, we must all agree on some ground rules before we go any further. These are in your packs, along with some forms for you to sign."

"No one mentioned anything about contracts," said the Griffton News publisher in a gruff voice. She was an American woman in her fifties with a red face and short blonde hair.

"It's just a formality, but we're all businesspeople, right? We know how the world works. We all stand to win big with this deal, people. I mean, look at this place. It's all mine now." She laughed aloud.

"I found an enormous plasma screen in one of the rooms upstairs and, like, ten or fifteen different types of ice cream in the freezer. I'm in paradise!"

The Chief of Police stared at her, his face unreadable.

"Anyway, you know the score. Sign your life away, and then let's talk turkey."

The officer opened his pack and started to read his papers.

⚮ 12345 ⚮

RACHEL STUMBLED ALONG A STRANGE ROAD, staring wildly around her. The swirling, violet, apocalyptic sky from her dreams hung above her. A bloodthirsty wind tore at her clothes, making her shiver. Trees and rocks seemed to hang in the air, but her hand moved through empty space when she tried to touch them.

At the edges of her peripheral vision, she could see massive superstructures. But these disappeared when she turned her head to look at them. Even the narrow path she walked on seemed insubstantial, with gaping holes leading down into an abyss. The top of an ice-capped mountain made of dark red rock appeared above her head. A blood-red moon presided over it all.

Confused and lonely, she walked a few paces, hugging her arms around her body. She jumped at an unfamiliar noise behind her but, spinning around, saw nothing.

The alien road stretched far ahead. It wound around a set of boulders the colour of dried blood, which overlaid a forest of fiery trees, like a double-exposure photograph that displayed the impossible. She decided to follow the long, narrow road that wound through this otherworldly valley. After all, the only way was forward now.

Rachel had left the stone head far behind her. It was identical to the one she had passed through on Griffton Cliff at the entrance to this world, but unlike the first doorway, this one seemed inert. It emitted no buzz of electricity, and there was no apparent way to enter it. She was stuck here now, with no way back.

❧ 12345 ❦

TANZANIA, East Africa.

Andwele Juma was nicknamed 'Ndege' because he was small and fast like a bird. He crouched at the edge of the Ngorongoro Crater, near where he and his family lived. Ndege was sitting before a broad tuft of thick yellow grass protruding like fingers around his bare toes.

The crater was one hundred and twenty-six square miles, six hundred and ten metres deep, and teeming with life. Living near the equator was good and hot. He loved the animals and the colours and did not take them for granted like his brothers.

Ndege squinted at the lush green and mustard carpet of trees and grass. A smoky blue cloud shadow brushed the base of the crater. He fancied he could even see a pink line at the dusty edge of the lake at the base of the crater. There were pink flamingos on the water far below, many thousands of them. Also, he knew there were black rhinos, elephants, and zebra. He often went down in his family's jeep.

He sensed he was not alone and turned around on his swift feet. A huge brown buffalo stared at him from a distance of a dozen feet, not moving. Its hairy back rippled in the breeze, and it snorted and gazed. It had massive, powerful shoulders. Its hoofs were caked with dry mud. Ndege tried to avoid its eyes as the East African sun bore down on him.

He pursed his lips and blew gently, and the buffalo retreated.

Safe again, he took some time to follow the edges of the crater with his eyes and mark its contours and colours. It really was beautiful and resonated inside his heart. He began to relax.

Just then, a creature jumped out at him from the long grass. It was a lizard or a spider monkey, he immediately thought. But as the creature landed on his arm, he saw it was a huge, furry animal like nothing he had seen before. It looked at him with round black button eyes.

Ndege watched it, feeling the weight on his arm and sniffing its leathery body.

"You are a strange beast," he told it. "I should show you to my brothers. They will know what you are."

That was when the creature attacked him. It brought out two great black wings and fixed its sharp, long teeth onto Ndege's middle finger. He roared with pain as it clamped its jaws down hard.

Ndege glimpsed the blood but fainted with the pain. He didn't even feel the monster dancing on his shoulder as it used his body to launch off into the afternoon skies with a screech and a flutter of reptilian wings.

Acknowledgments

I would like to thank my wife and children; my friends and broader family; my editors Jenny Burdett, Dan Lank, Natalie Smith, Peter Champneys, and Phoebe Mohamed; Jane and Carole at JAC Design; Louis at Lewis Design; my friends at The Book Whisperer; Clare King, Michael Thorn, and Reuben Lyons for his encouragement to "create culture!" To all of you and so many more—thank you for your support.

ABOUT THE AUTHOR

Joshua Raven has enjoyed thirty years as an international journalist, editor, business copywriter and media consultant. As a novelist he has been a featured author at the Dubai Emirates Airline Festival of Literature. And as a journalist and professional writer he has interviewed leading figures in business and technology, including Bill Gates and Michael Dell, and written for publications and businesses across the globe including The Times newspaper, Microsoft, Google and Facebook. Joshua lives in the South of England and enjoys people, music, cooking, reading, and travelling.

facebook.com/JoshuaRavenAuthor

x.com/RavenWrites

instagram.com/RavenWrites

linkedin.com/in/arif-mohamed-71b2831a

amazon.com/stores/Joshua-Raven/author/B0034O22RS

pinterest.com/joshuaraven75

ALSO BY JOSHUA RAVEN